"I want what daughter…"

"I need you to trust me with her." Rance's gaze snagged Larae's. "That I won't do anything to hurt her, try to exclude you when I spend time with her, or try to monopolize her. That I won't intentionally do anything to hurt you. Or your reputation."

"That all sounds good."

"And I need you to do the same. We need to raise her together and put her best interests first."

"I agree." Her heart did a painful flip-flop. She'd have to share her daughter from now on.

"I know I hurt you once. But I was a kid. I'm not anymore. How can I prove to you that I've changed?"

"Just don't let Jayda down. All I want is for her to be happy and loved."

"Me, too." He offered his hand. "Shake on it."

She wanted to trust his offer, but touching him always did funny things to her insides. Could she really trust this guy? Had he changed?

With all her Rance-entangled heart, she hoped so.

Shannon Taylor Vannatter is a stay-at-home mom/pastor's wife/award-winning author. She lives in a rural central Arkansas community with a population of around one hundred, if you count a few cows. Contact her at shannonvannatter.com.

Books by Shannon Taylor Vannatter

Love Inspired

Hill Country Cowboys

Hill Country Redemption

Texas Cowboys

Reuniting with the Cowboy
Winning Over the Cowboy
A Texas Holiday Reunion
Counting on the Cowboy

Love Inspired Heartsong Presents

Rodeo Ashes
Rodeo Regrets
Rodeo Queen
Rodeo Song
Rodeo Family
Rodeo Reunion

Visit the Author Profile page at Harlequin.com.

Hill Country Redemption

Shannon Taylor Vannatter

LOVE INSPIRED

INSPIRATIONAL ROMANCE

LOVE INSPIRED®
INSPIRATIONAL ROMANCE

Recycling programs
for this product may
not exist in your area.

ISBN-13: 978-1-335-48810-7

Hill Country Redemption

Copyright © 2020 by Shannon Taylor Vannatter

This edition published by arrangement with Harlequin Books S.A.

For questions and comments about the quality of this book, please contact us at CustomerService@Harlequin.com.

Love Inspired
22 Adelaide St. West, 40th Floor
Toronto, Ontario M5H 4E3, Canada
www.Harlequin.com

Printed in U.S.A.

I have no greater joy
than to hear that my children walk in truth.
—*3 John* 1:4

I dedicate this book to my husband.
I'm thoroughly enjoying our happily-ever-after
and I don't know what I'd do without your love
and support. God truly gave me a blessing in you.

Acknowledgments

I'm thankful for Texas Mom,
who always welcomes us to Medina for a visit,
even when she's sick with crud. I appreciate
Jennifer Slattery and Brenda S. Anderson for
reading my painfully awkward first drafts.
I'm grateful to Linda Fulkerson for being my
travel buddy to writers' conferences.
If not for her, I probably wouldn't be published.

Chapter One

The debit amounts blurred into one hemorrhaging red total, making Larae Collins's stomach clench. She closed the leather-bound ledger and handed it back to Denny as the porch swing's chains groaned. "I don't understand why Dad didn't tell me."

Her best friend's father, who'd been her dad's ranch foreman since forever, shook his head. "I reckon he didn't want to worry you."

A mixture of cattle lowing, bawling and stamping serenaded her. The sounds of home were so unlike her condo in Dallas with its constant traffic noise. This should have been the perfect spring break vacation she'd planned. Instead, she'd learned the property wasn't solvent. She needed to sell her childhood ranch—not get attached.

The buyer's low offer made sense now. And with her job downsized into history, what choice did she have?

"Mommy, I'm riding a pony!" Jayda, Larae's seven-year-old daughter, waved from astride Beans as a trusted ranch hand, who didn't know she'd been riding since was three, led the duo around the arena. The white-and-brown-splotched pinto pony had entertained children at the ranch for as long as Larae could remember.

"You're doing an excellent job!" Even on the pony, Jayda was tiny and had to keep pushing up the brim of the huge cowboy hat she wore to protect her from the relentless sun in Medina, Texas. Even though it was only the second week of March, it was almost eighty degrees.

Jayda resembled Larae and was small for her age, appearing to be younger than her seven years, which suited Larae. When Larae had left the ranch eight years ago, no one had known she was pregnant. Not even Jayda's father. All she had to do was accept the low offer for the ranch, then slip back to Dallas with her secret intact.

"The ranch has always turned huge profits." She shaded her eyes from the afternoon sun and peered up at Denny. He still smelled of hay and horse, with bronzed skin even more leathery than she remembered. "How did this happen?"

"We've had several dry years in a row, which meant more feed bought for the stock." Denny leaned a hip against the back-porch rail. "Cattle prices were down a few years, and several new horse ranches in the area are giving us stiff competition. All of it, combined with your daddy's illness, took a toll." He shifted his weight. "You gonna accept the offer?"

"I'm not sure." She had a nice nest egg, and her dad had left her a hefty inheritance. But with no income, she couldn't risk holding on to the ranch and paying to keep it going, especially since her daughter was depending on her. Yet, it would be an insult to take such a loss on the ranch her family had put blood and sweat into for three generations.

Her phone rang, and she dug it out of her pocket. Her former boss. "I need to get this."

"Take your time. I'll keep an eye on Little Miss." Denny straightened and strode toward the arena.

"Hello?"

"How's it going in Timbuktu?" Miles's tone didn't match his attempt at humor.

"Not as well as I hoped."

"I really hate to hear that. You've had a lot on you

lately, and I'm afraid I have more bad news." A heavy sigh. "I called that friend of mine at the rodeo in Bulverde—he just hired a new marketing director."

"Thanks for trying, Miles." Her heart sank. "I'll find something."

"I'm sorry, Larae. You're the best marketing director I ever worked with. I've a good mind to tell our new manager just what I think of her downsizing notions."

"Don't, Miles. She's just doing her job, cutting costs where she can. Keep your mouth shut and keep your job. You've only got a few more years until retirement. I'll be fine." She stood and paced the length of the porch.

"You let me know of any calls I need to make once you get your résumé out there. Some awesome rodeo will snap you up."

"Thanks, Miles."

"Don't be a stranger."

"I won't." She stepped off the porch and turned to face the back of the ranch house. All log beams and cedar siding. It had been her home for as long as she could remember. But now both of her parents were gone, the ranch was losing money, and she no longer had a job.

There weren't that many year-round rodeos in operation in Texas. What would she do now? She headed toward the arena.

She could live on her reserves if she unloaded the ranch. But rodeo was her passion and gave her flexible hours, with most of her work done from home, so she could always be there for Jayda. Her job had even allowed her dad to move in with them after his first stroke.

As she neared the arena, the ranch hand gave Jayda the reins, then stood in the center as her daughter circled, chattering nonstop. The child had never met a stranger.

Denny heard her approach and turned to face her, leaning against the arena rail with a grimace. "Bad news?"

It must have shown on her face.

"Look, Mommy. I think Beans likes me." Jayda circled near holding the reins.

"You're a natural." Larae waited until Jayda passed, then lowered her voice and summed up the phone call.

"You're too good at what you do to be unemployed for long." Denny scowled, gathering her into a fatherly hug. The sweet gesture made her miss her dad even more. Her eyes burned with a mixture of grief and frustration. But she wouldn't give in to it. She blinked away the moisture and pulled out of his arms, even though his embrace felt like home.

"Did I tell you Lexie's wanting to move home? She's trying to get a job at the clinic in Bandera."

"No, but I'm not surprised." Her best friend since childhood had always loved tiny Medina. "The city never fit her as well as it does me."

"You could stay here and run the ranch. Turn this place around."

"I don't know anything about ranching."

"Your staff does."

"But we're in the red." She scanned the dry, hardened ground, cracked from lack of rain. "If this drought keeps up, we'll stay there."

"A lot of the ranches in Bandera have opened dude ranches. The house is plenty big to accommodate guests."

"But this is Medina. You really think tourists would come here?"

"If we give them something to come for. And we have our very own marketing guru."

"Mommy, I don't want to go back to our condo." Jayda circled again, waving. "I want to stay here and ride Beans every day. Why did we never come here before?"

"I didn't realize you'd enjoy it so much." Partly true. But Larae had purposely stayed away for the last eight years to avoid Jayda's father. "It's only Sunday, sweetie.

We've got the rest of the week here. But how about we visit more often in the future?"

"I guess." The joy drained from her daughter's voice.

If she sold the ranch, there wouldn't be a *here* to visit. Jayda didn't know about the possible sale. Not yet. Larae hated keeping Jayda in the dark, but she hadn't expected her little girl to fall in love with the place so quickly.

Denny waited until Jayda passed out of earshot. "You could start your own rodeo. Here." He gestured to Jayda. "You've already got one vote to stay." He stuck his hand in the air. "I agree with Little Miss."

Larae chuckled. "Do you have any idea what that would entail? We'd have to construct a building, seating, the arena, hire a stock contractor and staff."

"You've already got the outdoor arena your daddy built for you back when you started barrel racing. A little upgrade, and you'd be all set. And without your job, you don't have anything to hightail it back to Dallas for." He scrutinized her. "Do you?"

When she'd shown up yesterday with Jayda in tow, Denny hadn't asked questions about her little girl's father. This was as close as he'd ever get.

"Nothing." Her cheeks heated. "But to turn a consistent profit, we'd have to go year-round indoor and get professionally sanctioned. And the ranch might go under before I can get all that done."

"Spruce up the outdoor facility to get things up and running while you build an indoor one."

Her own rodeo. And she could run it the way she wanted. Alcohol free—truly family friendly in honor of her mother. Living on her childhood ranch. It sure was tempting.

"Guess who lives next door?"

"Who?"

"A stock contractor."

"You're making that up."

"Naw, I'm shooting straight with you. It's like some-body wants you here. And I'm not talking about me or Little Miss." Denny looked up at the sky.

Larae followed his gaze. *Do you want me here, Lord?* A sense of peace settled over her. More than she'd known since she'd left here at eighteen.

And the thing that had kept her away—Rance Shepherd—was still traveling the rodeo circuit, last she'd heard. Her father had tried to talk her into moving back over the years, but she'd been knee-deep in her job—the job she didn't have anymore. And she hadn't wanted to face questions about Jayda's father. She still didn't.

"I can see your wheels spinning." Denny grinned. "Why don't you go on over next door and put some feel-ers out? You might even remember our new neighbor. He worked for—"

Jayda circled again. "Isn't she pretty, Mommy?"

"She is, sweetie. But not as pretty as you." She winked at her daughter. "I have an errand to run. You do what Denny tells you, and I'll be right back."

"Okay."

"It'd be right nice if you and Little Miss stayed put," Denny said.

"I'm just checking things out." She headed down the drive to cut across to the ranch house next door. Who was this stock contractor? The Long family had lived there for as far back as she could remember. Maybe one of their sons or grandsons owned it now. Denny had been about to tell her when Jayda had interrupted. She should have stuck around long enough to get a name.

The Texas sun prickled her skin as she opened the side gate to the Longs' yard. With aged graying wood siding, the house looked just as it always had, and the wide, in-viting front porch still beckoned her to sit a spell.

Something slammed into her backside. Screaming, she

flailed, then sprawled on the parched earth, barely missing a collision with the bottom step.

Rance bolted around the house. A second scream
erupted. In the yard, a petite blonde sat in the dust near
the porch. With Gruff nibbling at her shoe.

"Gruff, what did you do?"

She rolled away and tried to scramble to her feet.

He grabbed the water soaker gun from the porch,
flooded the goat and elicited another scream from the
blonde.

"Baa!" Gruff reared up on his back hooves, then disappeared around the side of the house.

"He's gone. Just a big baby." He reached to help her
up. "Are you hurt?"

She pushed to her feet, ignoring his hand, then wiped
off her seat and brushed at the grime on her light-colored
jeans. Her right leg was soaked, thanks to him. She looked
up and revealed the bluest eyes that had ever left a hole
in his heart. His breath caught in his lungs.

Larae's gaze turned icy. "Rance? What are you doing
here?"

"I could ask the same of you." He tried for natural,
but his tone came off stilted. He'd only moved back because Larae Collins had left for the city ages ago. And
stayed there. Surely she was only visiting, here to sell her
childhood ranch now that her dad was gone. "Sorry about
Gruff. I borrowed him from a friend to clean up all the
dead, out-of-control flower beds for me."

"Leave it to you to keep an attack goat in the yard."

"I wasn't expecting visitors. Sorry for the dowsing,
too. I'm trying to teach him manners with the master
blaster." He managed a tight smile. "Guess I need to work
on my aim."

"His playing could hurt someone. Especially a child."
She frowned.

"Well, it's a good thing I don't have any of those."

Something snapped in her eyes. She turned and stalked away. Flung the gate open, slammed it shut. It automatically latched as she marched out of sight.

What had he said to rile her so? Maybe it was just him in general? After all, he'd broken up with her out of the blue. She still didn't know why, and he couldn't tell her. But that was eight years ago.

He shot after her, through the gate, and caught up with her halfway down her long driveway. "Did you need something?"

"Never mind." She ignored him as he matched her stride. As if he wasn't even there.

"Well, at least let me buy you a new pair of jeans."

"They'll wash, and they're not designer."

One of the reasons he'd initially liked her as a teen. They'd gone to a private school full of rich and spoiled kids. Yet Larae had never been snooty or had to have the best of everything, even though her family could've afforded it and then some.

"At least tell me what you came over for? Were you looking for one of the Long girls?" Even though the Longs had been a hardworking ranch family struggling to make ends meet and their kids went to public school, Larae had befriended the middle daughter.

She stopped and faced him. "Fine. I came to talk to the stock contractor. Do you work for him?"

"Actually." He hesitated. "You're looking at him."

Chapter Two

"Oh." Larae looked like she might swallow her tongue, then took off along her drive again.

Had she become like her dad during her years in the city—never expecting Rance to amount to much? Did she think he was destined to be hired help for the rest of his days? If only she knew Remington blood ran through his veins. And it was boiling right about now.

He should have revealed his family tree back when her dad had tried to get rid of him. That was years ago, but it stung just the same. No one would ever think he was after her money—or anyone else's—again.

"Know somebody who needs a stock contractor?" He caught up with her in a few strides.

"Me. Maybe. I was thinking of starting a rodeo on the ranch."

"A rodeo? Here in Medina?"

"I'm rethinking things." Her steps sped up.

He stayed right with her in spite of her attempts to escape. "Because I'm the stock contractor?" It was kind of fun watching her squirm.

"I'm just undecided on what to do with the ranch right now. I should think it over before making any rash decisions."

"Because anything to do with me would obviously be rash." Sarcasm coated his words.

She stopped, whirled to face him. "Definitely." Her chin went up a notch. "I doubt you'll stick with this new venture for long since you can't seem to commit to anything. Or anyone. If I start a rodeo, I won't be calling you." She stalked down the driveway.

"Good," he hollered after her. "You know me, I probably won't even be here by then anyway." Now why had he said that? Because she'd gone all snooty on him, and under no circumstances did he want her to think he was still pining for her.

Same silky blond hair, fire and ice eyes, slender build. Same temper. Wrapped in a tiny, mesmerizing, exasperating package.

The last thing he needed was to live next door to the only woman who had the ability to rearrange his heart into a million jagged pieces. He couldn't possibly work with her. Could he? Since he'd just bought the business from his former boss, he badly needed a rodeo to boost his résumé.

He trudged back to the house. As he entered the yard, Gruff innocently munched on the last crunchy brown vine trailing up the porch column.

"I think you've caused enough mischief, mister." He slipped a rope around the goat's neck and led him out the gate toward his smallest stock trailer. "Next time I need yard work, I'll borrow one of your lady friends. You're officially fired and going home."

He got the typical "baa" in response. Surely Larae wasn't planning to live here. She was a city girl now—had been for years. She'd get her rodeo up and running, then waltz back to her fancy Dallas life and let her ranch hands run it for her.

Tomorrow, he'd go over there, make peace and land his

first official gig since striking out on his own. He couldn't let this opportunity pass—Larae or no Larae.

Monday morning, Larae strolled toward the barn, where a tall man with a wiry build chatted with Denny. Low murmurs, the laughter of ranch hands, cattle moos and horse nickers echoed around. Sounds she hadn't realized she missed. Until now.

Her little girl was still twisted among the sheets, sound asleep when Larae had left. Jayda knew the rules. Stay in the house or yard, no opening of gates or going inside the cattle fences. If she awoke with Larae gone, she'd end up in the kitchen with Stella, Denny's wife.

With Rance right next door, Larae couldn't possibly stay. Her insides coiled. Should she tell him about Jayda? He was obviously just as selfish, carefree and likely to run off to the rodeo as he'd been back in school. Something her daughter didn't need. She couldn't let him reject Jayda the way he'd rejected her. He had the right to know, but he didn't deserve to know.

"Morning." Denny's drawl greeted her as soon as she was within hearing distance. "The metal building guy I told you about is here." He waved her over. "You remember Carson Glover."

"I do." Wow. Denny didn't waste any time in his campaign to convince her to stay. "I remember when he was twelve, trailing around after his daddy mucking stalls for us and pulling my ponytail when nobody was looking." He was five years her junior with a full-on crush on her.

"Guilty as charged. But I'm all grown-up and married with a baby on the way now." Carson shook her hand. "Good to see you. Heard you're considering starting a rodeo in the old arena and building an indoor facility on the property."

"I'm still in the thinking stage."

"Where were you thinking of putting it?"

She scanned the property and blew out a breath. "I haven't even thought that far. Where do you suppose would be a good place?" She pointed to the field with rolling hills behind the barn. "Maybe there?"

"Could be done. But it would take a lot of foundation work. The more level the ground, the better." He gestured to the field that was left of the barn, beside the outdoor arena. "We could build a concession stand and bathrooms for the outdoor arena and eventually incorporate them into the indoor building."

"That could work."

"What size?"

She shrugged. "Typical indoor arena size."

He grinned. "Tell you what… I'll do some research and find out what size that is, draw up some specs and get back with you."

"That sounds perfect."

"Thanks for coming." Denny shook Carson's hand.

"Thanks for thinking of me." He turned toward his dust-coated once-black Cadillac in the drive.

The rodeo could work whether she stayed or not. She could get it going, then go back to Dallas.

To do what? The rodeo in Mesquite was out of the picture. It was fully staffed and comfortably set up, and it ran only three months each year anyway. Besides, she couldn't let Rance think she was running away because of him. He needed to think he didn't matter to her one way or the other.

But she couldn't hire him. Her heart couldn't survive working with him. And she had to keep him away from Jayda. Maybe she was right about him, that he wouldn't stick with stock contracting for the long run. He'd leave, and this constant pressure in her chest would dissipate.

"Here comes just the guy you need." Denny gestured behind her.

As if on cue, Rance strode down her drive, headed straight for her. Had he gotten even better looking in the past eight years? Definitely. A shadow of dark hair edged his cowboy hat, bottle green eyes sparkling in the sun, cleft chin. Oh, if only a sinkhole would open up in the baked earth and swallow him whole.

He and Carson spoke in passing as she tried to come up with a reason to escape. What if Jayda woke up and came outside looking for her? What if Rance saw his daughter?

Calm down. Jayda didn't look like him, and everyone assumed she was five or six instead of seven. Her secret was safe.

Rance's steps stalled a few feet away from Larae. Even after all these years, she still held him captive. "Since Carson was here, I assume you're going ahead with the rodeo."

"He's getting me some stats to help me decide."

"Well, I'm here to convince you to hire me if this thing gets real."

"Why would I do that?" She hooked her thumbs in her pockets and peered up at him.

"Because I'm guessing all the stock contractors you know are in the Dallas/Fort Worth area. Using them would cost more. I'm right next door—willing and able— at a lower price. And you're in the thinking stage of this rodeo to make a profit, right?"

"I know it's none of my beeswax, Larae." Denny propped his boot on the fence rail. "I know you want an experienced contractor and Rance is just getting started. But he knows his stuff. You're shooting yourself in the foot if you don't hire him. There aren't any other stock contractors outside of San Antonio."

Way to put her on the spot. "There you have it, Denny's stamp of approval."

"Just my way of watching over you, like your daddy

would want." Denny headed for the barn. "I best get to work."

"Thanks, Denny." Larae leaned her elbows on the fence and kept her gaze on the foreman's retreating back, instead of looking at Rance. "How did Denny become your biggest fan?"

"Several men from the area eat breakfast at the Old Spanish Trail just about every morning. Tex Warren, my dad, and Denny included."

"So he thinks you're awesome because your dad does?"

"Tex Warren is Ty's dad and Clay's granddad. Both Warrens won the Championship Bull Riding title four times apiece. Tex was impressed with some of my bulls." But no matter who his bulls awed, Larae would remain unconvinced. "The rodeo is a great idea. I want the job. Do you have any idea of how much stock you'll need? You do your marketing and publicity thing. I'll handle the livestock."

She faced him and propped her hands on her hips. "How do you know what I do?"

"I trained under the stock contractor who supplied the rodeo you work for."

One eyebrow lifted. Aware of how smoothly his old boss's stock operation ran for her rodeo, she couldn't help but be impressed. Could she?

"I can check with Carson on the arena sizes he's running, then give you numbers, cost and prospectus for each."

"You can?"

"What? You didn't think I knew big words like *prospectus*?"

"Actually." She pursed her lips. "I must admit I'm impressed. I didn't know you handled the business end of things. I figured you tended to the cattle and let somebody else crunch numbers."

A compliment? "Listen, can we call a truce and work

together on this? I really think your rodeo could be successful here. Area businesses could use a new influx of tourist dollars. Keeping costs low would allow the competitors a bigger purse, which would line the cowboys' pockets and put your rodeo on the map. Everybody wins."

She blew out a sigh that ruffled the long layers framing her face. "I'm sorry for the way I acted yesterday. I just wasn't expecting you, and I lashed out. If we're to work together, we need to forget the past and focus on the rodeo." Her glance strayed toward the house as if she had somewhere to be…or was waiting for someone.

Was she married? His gaze dipped to her left hand, then back to her face. No ring. "I'm in. I'll run some numbers and get back to you. Tomorrow?"

"Sure. Just give me a call. We still have the landline, and I'll give Carson a heads-up on working with you." Her gaze snagged on something, and her eyes widened.

He followed her line of vision. A little girl skipped in their direction.

"I have to go." Larae bolted toward the child.

Chapter Three

Rance frowned. A child?

Denny entered the arena with a bay mare as Larae hustled the little girl back to the house.

"Who's that?"

"Larae's girl. Spitting image of her mama, that one."

He swallowed hard. Could the child be his? If so, she'd be a little over seven years old. This child looked smaller. "How old is she?"

"Five or six from the looks of her."

His insides stilled. Larae would have told him if the child belonged to him. This meant that while he'd been mourning his first love all those years ago, she'd moved on to someone else. To be honest, he wasn't sure he'd ever really moved on from her at all. "Who's her daddy? Is Larae married?"

"I don't rightly know."

"You've worked for her dad forever, and she's your daughter's best friend. How could you not know?"

"They were both closemouthed about Larae after she left, and I'm not one to pry. I didn't know about the youngun' until they showed up here a few days ago." Denny gave him the once-over. "Why are you so interested?"

"I'm not. Just curious." Denny didn't have a clue they'd been an item back in high school. No one had because she knew her dad wouldn't approve. "I didn't know she had a child, that's all. I'll see you later." With his heart in his boots, he trudged toward home.

The thought of her with anyone else put a painful twist in his gut. He'd given her up for the sake of her relationship with her dad, but he'd never thought about her falling for someone else.

His phone rang. He fished it out of his pocket, saw the name on the screen and accepted the call. "Hey, Dad."

"How's the stock contracting business going, son?"

"Slow. I might have a job, but it's complicated."

"Complicated how?"

He filled his dad in on the Larae situation.

"I see." His father let out a long whistle. "Hence the complicated maybe job."

"It was like I was seventeen again."

"You still love her?"

"Now, I didn't say that."

"Yet you did, by not saying it. Go get the job and the girl."

"Even if I wanted her, there's more to it than that." But he couldn't get into it, since he'd never told his parents why they broke up. If he had, his dad would have confronted Ray Collins, and the whole town would have heard about it. Even Larae.

"Is she involved with someone else?"

"I'm not sure." A tight band settled in his chest. "She has a child."

"Hmm. Well, find out if the father is still in the picture and go from there. But be careful, son. I was there the first time Larae Collins broke your heart."

"It wasn't her fault, Dad." Rance opened the gate to his yard, now free of tangled vines thanks to the attack goat he'd borrowed yesterday.

"You keep saying that, but you won't say anything else."

"It's—"

"Complicated. I know. Keep me in the loop, will ya? Your mom wants to talk to you. Here she is."

"Hi, Mom. I'm eating fine. I fixed a pot of chili last night."

"Well, you won't starve, but that's not very healthy—all that red meat." Since learning that her husband had high cholesterol, she'd become a health food expert.

"I used venison." Only because he liked it better, but maybe it would satisfy her just the same.

"Oh, good. You can't imagine how much fat a lean meat can cut. You can try ground turkey if you run out of venison."

"I've got a freezer full, so I'm good."

"All right. You'll come visit soon, right?"

"I will, Mom. And y'all are welcome here anytime. Love you." He slipped the phone back in his pocket, stomped his boots on the slatted wood porch and stepped inside. He loved his parents, but he couldn't concentrate on his mom's chatter right now.

Larae had a child. His brain kept looping back to that.

What if there was a man in her life? His heart stilled at the thought. It might just fix everything. It would hurt to see her with someone else. But if she was married, he'd have to get over her.

"I sure hope Lexie moves back soon." Stella wiped down the kitchen counters. She hadn't changed a bit. Still tall and thin, with warm laugh lines around her eyes.

"Me, too." Seated at the breakfast bar, Larae finished off her eggs.

"Our Lexie?" Jayda asked, pushing a stalk of broccoli around her plate.

"Remember, I told you Denny and Stella are her parents."

"But I didn't know she was gonna move here. I'm excited."

"Me too, Little Miss." Stella winked at Jayda. Denny's wife had happily cooked for staff and watched their children for as long as Larae could remember.

The knocker sounded at the heavy front door.

"It's awful early for visitors." Stella pushed a strand of hair away from her face and tried to secure it back in the bun at the nape of her neck. "And the hands don't usually knock."

"I'll get it." Larae got up from her perch at the granite-lined breakfast bar and pointed a stern finger at Jayda. "You stay put and eat the rest of your omelet. It's good for you." The cheese sauce probably took away from its benefits, but broccoli wrapped in egg was the only way to get veggies down Jayda.

"I'll make sure she does." Stella shot her a wink.

"Thanks." She hurried to the front door and swung it open. Carson stood on the threshold with a thick folder under his arm.

"Is this a good time? I have numbers for you."

"You're fast." She gestured him toward the great room so she could keep an eye on Jayda in the adjoining kitchen. "Come on in."

"I've got specs on three different sizes." He settled on the cowhide sofa and set his folder on the coffee table. "We'll call them Building A, B and C. A is small, just meets the regulations. B is the most common. C is more your Fort Worth or Mesquite size."

"So I'd need to go with C if I wanted to get pro certified?" Nerves danced through her.

"Definitely C."

"I figure go big or go home."

"Alrighty then." He flipped past several papers.

She scanned the spreadsheet to the bottom total. Not as much as she'd expected. "If we do this, how soon are we talking?"

"We could break ground in a few weeks and have your building ready in two months."

"And what about the arena part?"

"That's out of my line of expertise, so I'm afraid I can't help you there."

"Well, this is encouraging." She was well aware of how much revenue a good rodeo could bring in, especially if she could get certified for pro events. It would be enough to permanently keep the ranch well in the black.

"Thank you for putting this together, Carson. I'll look over it some more and get back with you."

"Not a problem." He stood, and she followed him to the foyer.

If she did this, she'd have to hire Rance. Otherwise, she'd only look stupid. Or still hung up on him. Maybe she could get the arrangements in place, then go back to Dallas and oversee the rodeo from afar. Whatever it took to avoid Rance.

The knocker sounded again.

"Next." Carson grinned as he opened the door.

Rance stood on the stoop. His gaze pinged back and forth between them, landed on Carson and narrowed. "You?"

"Me what?"

Surely Rance didn't think she was involved with Carson. Why would he care? "Carson was here going over numbers for a possible arena building."

"I was just leaving."

"Thanks again, Carson." He exited, but she didn't step aside to let Rance in, willing Jayda to take her sweet time finishing her broccoli. "Can I help you?"

"I brought my numbers, too."

"It'll have to wait. I don't do business at my home. We'll have to set up a time to meet."

"Hmm, let's see what's wrong with this picture. Your

office is at your house, and you met with Carson about business."

"Fine." She backed away and then ushered him through the formal living room. "But not here. Let's go to Dad's office."

In the doorway facing her father's massive desk, she stopped. The room still smelled of his Old Spice cologne. She'd spent half her childhood in the wood-paneled room but had never sat in his cushy executive chair. Just the sight of it put a knot in her throat.

"How about the table?" Rance set his file on the long conference table.

"Yes." Did he understand her hesitation, feel for her grief?

"I was sorry to hear about your dad."

Sympathy from him would surely undo her. She cleared her throat. "Thanks. What have you got?"

He opened the folder. The spreadsheet listed all his stock, along with his fee. "Do you know which size you're going with yet?"

"The biggest." She rattled off the specs Carson had given her.

"Good choice." He pulled a loose sheet and handed it to her. "This is what you'll need. The fees listed beside each of my bulls, broncs and steers is what I get every time they leave the chute. They're priced according to bloodlines, and I'll handle all the transport. I took the liberty of contacting an acquaintance who builds arenas. He said he'd work with Carson and have your rodeo up and running a month after the building is finished."

Surprisingly thorough. "Did you think to ask him about updating the outdoor arena until the building is functional?"

"If he breaks ground next week, the weather holds, and inspectors don't give him trouble, he said three weeks. A month at the most."

"Wow." Fast enough to turn the ranch around.

"His estimates are in the file, too. It's a great idea, Larae. There aren't any indoor rodeos in this area except in San Antonio. And none them are year-round. I hope you'll get past the thinking stage."

"It's a lot to take on."

"How long are you here for?"

"It was supposed to only be a week." But that was before her new manager decided to handle marketing, too, leaving Larae jobless and bent on selling the ranch, even at a loss.

"You could hire someone to oversee things when you go back."

If she went back. "I've thought about that, too." She closed the file. But right now she needed to get rid of him. Not even Jayda had ever made broccoli last this long. "Thank you for putting this together. I'll get back with you if I decide to move forward."

He stayed seated. His jaw ticked as if he had more to say. She stood to give him the hint. He reluctantly followed her lead.

"All right then—" he turned and opened the door "—just let me know."

"Mommy, I ate all of my broccoli. Can I have my chocolate milk now?" Jayda stopped when she saw Rance. "Oh. Hi." Never shy.

At the moment, Larae wished she was.

"Broccoli for breakfast?" Rance grimaced. "I'm Rance. An old friend of your mom's."

Larae's heart did somersaults against her ribs. He'd gotten a glimpse of Jayda yesterday and obviously learned she was Larae's daughter. But then, anybody would know that by looking at her. Just as long as he didn't figure out anything else, everything would be fine.

"It was in an omelet. I'm Jayda."

"It's nice to meet you, Jayda."

"You can have your milk, and a cookie, too." *Just go.* Rance had said only a few days ago that it was a good thing he didn't have kids, and who knew how long he'd stick with this stock contracting thing? Hopefully long enough to get her rodeo going. Then he could run off for the rodeo circuit again, none the wiser. Footloose and fancy-free just the way he liked it.

"Everybody thinks I'm five or six—"

"Jayda, go have your cookies now. You can have three."

"Three." Jayda grinned. "You never let me have three." Rance chuckled.

"Just this once. Since you ate all your broccoli."

"But I'm not finished. I wanted to tell Rance I'm really seven."

"Jayda." Her daughter's name ripped from her throat. It was too late.

Rance's grin slipped away. His eyes widened, then narrowed as he inspected Jayda.

"What, Mommy?"

"I've warned you about talking to strangers, haven't I?" It was the only thing she could come up with.

"I thought that only counted when you weren't around."

"You're right. I forgot." At the moment she was forgetting how to breathe.

"You're seven?" The wonder in Rance's tone put a hitch in her throat.

"Uh-huh. I'm just small for my age. Mommy said she was the same way until she hit a growth spurt when she was twelve."

"Larae—" Rance's gaze snagged on hers as he ground her name out between his teeth. "We need to talk."

Chapter Four

In and out. Rance concentrated on breathing. Jayda's rounded eyes flitted back and forth between him and Larae. How could she have kept this from him?

"Go have your cookies now, Jayda. I'll be done here in just a minute."

"Okay, Mommy." Jayda glanced back at him one more time.

He'd obviously scared her, practically growling at Larae. He forced a smile.

Jayda slipped from the room.

"I—" Larae said.

"She's mine."

Larae closed her eyes. "Yes."

"Why didn't you tell me?"

"Because by the time, I found out—" her hand went to her middle "—you were dating Veronica Belmont."

Only to convince her they were finished. For her sake. While he'd been doing what he thought was right, to keep her relationship with her father intact, she'd been pregnant with his child.

His blood boiled. "Did your dad know?"

"Yes."

But she'd fled to Dallas. "Did he kick you out?"

"Of course not. He was very supportive."

If only she knew. The old coot. "He sent you to Dallas to keep me in the dark."

"You'd proven you weren't ready for fatherhood."

"You had no right to make that call."

"We'd broken up. You'd moved on. I wasn't about to obligate you. To risk you coming back to me." She jabbed her thumb toward her chest. "Because of duty. It was my decision to go to college in Dallas and stay to pursue my career."

"To hide. From me."

"And from wagging tongues." She hugged herself. "I did what I thought was best. For my daughter."

"Our daughter." He sank into a chair as all his anger drained away. What good did it do to be mad at a dead man? "I loved you, Larae. I'd have dropped everything for you. Quit the rodeo and married you." In spite of her dad.

"If you loved me so much—" her words dripped sarcasm "—then why did you break up with me?"

He wouldn't explain. He couldn't skew her memories of her dad, not with her still grieving his loss. "I didn't think I was good enough for you."

She scoffed. "Well, you were good enough for Veronica Belmont. And Prudence Hancock. And who knows who else. Face it, Rance. You were a playboy working your way through all the rich girls in school."

Only to convince Larae he didn't love her. To save her relationship with her father—the man who'd stood by and watched, effectively ripping away Rance's chance to be a father.

"That's not who I am."

"If you say so. But the fact remains, while you've been doing whatever you've been doing for the last eight years, I've been making adult decisions and taking care of my daughter. And she's waiting for me in the kitchen, so you can go now. We didn't need you then, and we don't need you now. Please just go." She moved to the door, obviously expecting him to do her bidding.

"No."

"Please, Rance." Her voice was softer now. Pleading. Her posture changed and she melted into herself. "You don't owe us anything. We'll move back to Dallas. I'll get the rodeo going from there, and we'll be out of your hair."

"I can't ignore this. She's my responsibility."

"She doesn't have to be. I'm fine financially. And I don't have to keep the ranch. I can unload it and not spend the funds I have on the rodeo."

"That's not what I mean, Larae. I intend to support her financially. But it's more than that. I have a daughter. And whether you think she needs me or not, I can't just pretend she doesn't exist. She's part of me."

Her eyes watered up. "The best part."

"I'm glad—" his throat closed up "—to know you still think there's good in me."

"I loved you. Once." She blinked the moisture away.

"We can work this out. I need to be in her life."

"Fine." She swallowed hard. "But you can't just waltz into her life, get her used to you, and then traipse off after some woman. Or rodeo. And leave Jayda behind and heartbroken."

"I won't." He spewed out a sigh. "I was mad the other day when I popped off about not being here long, but I didn't mean it. I'm here. For the long run."

"What about the rodeo? You've been a bronc rider for as long as I can remember."

"I'm not as young as I was." He rubbed his injured shoulder. "It started hurting more than it used to. And I missed home. So I moved to Fort Worth three years ago when I got an opportunity to get into stock contracting. I'm done with competing. I started my own business so I could come back to Medina."

"I just wish…"

"What do you wish?" That they'd never broken up? That they'd gotten married, raised their daughter together?

"That I could trust you. To stay. To fully commit to Jayda."

"You can. That guy in high school, the one who dumped you, the one who went on and dated all those other girls—that wasn't me. I'm a Christian now. I even attend church."

"I've seen how churches work, and Christians are still all too human." She rolled her eyes with a scoff. "Regardless of who you are, we seem to bring out the worst in each other."

"Then let's change that." He stood and gently touched her chin until she looked up at him again. "You can trust me now. If you move back to Dallas, I'll move there, too. I want to be Jayda's father. I need to be her father. For the rest of her life."

She took in a deep breath and nodded. "Just give me some time to break it to her."

Wait? Even though he wanted to rush into the kitchen, gather Jayda in his arms, tell her he was her father and start making up for the time they'd lost? Patience had never been his best trait.

"I'll come back tomorrow."

"Maybe a little more time than that?"

"How much time could it possibly take to say, 'This is your father'?"

"I'd like to ease into it slowly, then take time to let it sink in before you blast into her life."

"Please don't put it off, Larae. You know I don't do waiting well." His feet felt leaden as he walked to the door. Everything in him wanted to bolt for the kitchen. He put one foot in front of the other till he reached the front door and stepped outside. Though everything had changed in an instant, he'd go back to his empty, lonely house. And wait.

If only he'd committed to Christ back in high school, maybe he would have made better decisions. Maybe he could have witnessed to her and they wouldn't have had a child out of wedlock. Maybe he could have eventually won her dad over, proved himself as a stock contractor. Had Jayda after they were married. Done things right.

Things could have gone so differently. Regrets piled high. But Jayda wasn't one of them. She was the blessing that came out of their mistakes, and he couldn't wait to be her dad. Maybe he could find out what Larae had against Christians and witness to her. If they could get on the same page spiritually, everything would be easier.

He dug his phone out of his pocket, scrolled to his father's number and stopped. Despite the circumstances, his parents would be thrilled to learn they were grandparents. But they'd want to see Jayda right away. And they might hold Larae's silence against her. He couldn't tell them. Not yet.

Things didn't need to get any more complicated than they already were. After he and Larae found their footing with each other—once Jayda knew who he was and things smoothed out a bit—then he'd tell his parents. He slipped the phone back into his pocket.

His old feelings for Larae had to remain buried deep. No one knew he had big-money family ties. If he let himself fall for her again, some people would think he was a gold digger, just as her father had. He had to make a success of his new business before he could even think about anything more than coparenting with her.

Mental and physical exhaustion threatened to overtake Larae. She'd barely slept last night. After all these years of holding her secret tight, Rance knew the truth. Her future was uncharted territory. Everything would change. She'd have to share Jayda.

Perched on the porch swing, her gaze went to the arena, where Jayda was riding Beans. She hadn't broached the subject of Rance with Jayda yet, and she had to figure out a way. He wouldn't be patient forever.

How would she break the news to her little girl? *Sweetie, I've been keeping your father away from you all these years because I thought he was a jerk. But now, maybe he's not. Or maybe he is and he's just pretending he isn't.*

At the moment, she needed to focus on the rodeo. The list of phone numbers blurred before her eyes. She should be calling friends and former colleagues to find potential rodeo staff—bullfighters, chute bosses, announcers. The list went on. She couldn't build a rodeo if she couldn't staff it. So much to do and so much on her mind. She couldn't seem to function.

"There you are."

She jumped at the sound of Rance's voice. He rounded the side of the house, took the steps in one long lope and settled beside her on the swing as if she'd invited him.

"Whatcha doing?" He glanced at the phone numbers in her file.

"What are you doing here? I thought you were going to wait. I haven't told her anything yet."

"Yeah, about that… That doesn't mean I have to stay away, does it? What's wrong with me being around, letting her get used to me, then telling her who I am? Don't worry. I won't say anything." Jayda's giggle caught his attention, and he looked toward the arena. His jaw went slack. "But I don't think I can stay away." He stood.

"Wait." She grabbed his arm. Muscles flexed under her fingertips, and electricity sparked between them. Her hand slipped away. "I guess I'll have to put up with you since you're obviously not going to do what I say. But

I'm not comfortable with you being around her without me. Yet. I'm afraid you'll let something slip. And I can't drop everything and hang out with y'all today. I have calls to make."

"Can I help with the calls?"

"Maybe." She gestured to her list. "I called Carson and told him to get started on the indoor building and contacted the arena company you recommended to spruce the outdoor site into shape. But now I need to call all my rodeo contacts. I'm trying to find staff and hoping my contacts can make recommendations."

"So you're staying? Going ahead with the rodeo idea?"

She let out a sigh. Might as well come clean. "My job in Dallas got downsized and my lease on our condo is up in May, so I can't really think of anything we have to go back for. Jayda loves it here. The rodeo idea is growing on me. And you're here." Her voice cracked. "If you're going to be a part of her life, I figure we should stay put." At least for now.

"I know this is hard. But I won't let you down. Not this time." He reached over and closed her file. "I have a better idea on how to find rodeo staff, though."

"How?"

"You're a marketing guru. Make flyers announcing your rodeo with a list of employment opportunities. Put tabs with your number on the bottom for interested parties to call for details. You can put the info on the radio in the community announcements also."

"Why didn't I think of that?"

"Your brain's on overload."

"But if I call my rodeo contacts, I can get references."

"This way you'll find out who's available and interested. You can still use your contacts to vet any calls you get from flyers. And I know lots of rodeo workers, so I can help you hire the best."

"Maybe it would speed up the process."

"Tell you what, let Jayda finish her ride while we go inside and put together flyers. Once we get them printed, we'll drive into town and the surrounding areas to hang flyers. The three of us."

"And you'll still just be my friend from high school?"

"Until you say different."

"Deal." She offered her hand. At the fiery touch of his fingers, she wished she hadn't. She jerked away and stood. "We better get busy then."

He hesitated, his gaze riveted on the arena. "Can we talk to Jayda first? Just for a minute."

That was the last thing she wanted, but there was no getting around it anymore. "Sure."

"Really?" His face lit up like a kid's on a rare snow day in Texas.

Had Jayda already wound herself around his heart? "As long as you don't tell her anything or do anything weird—like hug her or cry."

"I don't cry."

But if she didn't know better, she'd say his green eyes were a little too shiny.

"Let's go." He blinked a few times and stood.

Had he actually changed or was he only acting like he cared, the way he had back in high school? Her legs weren't long enough to keep up with him, and he beat her to the arena.

"Hey, Mommy." Jayda waved.

"Hey, Pumpkin. You remember Rance?"

"Mmm-hmm." The little girl looked at him, uncertain.

"I'm helping your mom with some work here at the ranch. Sorry I was kind of grumpy yesterday. I'm not usually like that."

"It's okay. I get grumpy when I'm tired."

"You sure ride well. Did you have a pony in Dallas?"

"No. But Mommy started taking me to the stables when I was three."

"I can tell."

Every nerve ending Larae owned stood on end. "Listen Sweetie, Rance and I are going to Grandpa's office to get some work done. In an hour or so, we'll go hang flyers in Medina, Bandera and a couple of other towns. You can go with us."

"Flyers for what?"

"I'm thinking about starting a rodeo here on the ranch."

"Our own rodeo." Jayda's mouth made a small O. "That sounds like fun."

And a lot of work. "Denny, just send her inside when you get ready. She'll keep you out here all day if you let her." Larae pointed her finger at Jayda. "Just a few more minutes. Mr. Denny has work to do. And once you come inside, you can watch cartoons, or hang out with Ms. Stella, or come in the office with us."

"Okay, Mommy."

"Rance, you coming?"

With a wave to Jayda, he regretfully turned to follow her.

This was gonna be harder than she'd thought. She'd have to figure out a way to tell Jayda who he was. Soon.

Chapter Five

~~~

Rance stood at the window. He'd watched Jayda until Denny had helped her dismount. His daughter. Surreal. And yet very real. And woven into his heart in the very short time of knowing about her.

Realizing she was in the house somewhere had him wired, wishing he could be with her instead of stuck in the office.

"How's this look?" Larae leaned back in her chair.

He strolled up behind her and bent to peer over her shoulder. Her apple scent invaded his space. The same scent she'd worn in school. He never could determine if it was her hair or skin or both.

"What do you think?"

He focused on the screen. "I don't know. You're the marketing guru."

"Would it get your attention enough to read and see if stock contractor was listed?"

The word *Rodeo* was in huge print, followed by *"Do you love rodeos? Imagine a rodeo in Medina. Every weekend, year-round. Let's make it happen."* A bullet list of job openings followed, with "call this number if interested" tabs at the bottom. Rodeo graphics bordered the flyer.

"Yes. And if I wasn't already hired, I'd be disappointed to see it not listed."

"But what if I can't get this thing off the ground? I don't want to false advertise or get anybody's hopes up."

"It's not something you can waffle back and forth on. You already hired workers to whip the arena into shape and break ground on the indoor facility. And you're really good at this. With your marketing tactics, I think your rodeo can succeed."

"Thanks." She clicked the print tab. Seconds later, the printer hummed out the first copy. "I figure we can go to Fredericksburg, Kerrville, Hondo and Vanderpool, too. We can take separate vehicles if you don't want to go that far."

"We can ride together. Nothing else to do until we get this rodeo up and going. As long as we'll be back in time for church service at six."

"Oh wow, it's Wednesday, isn't it?" She checked her watch. "It's not quite ten. We'll be back in plenty of time for you to go."

"Why don't y'all come to church with me?"

"No thanks."

"If you don't mind me asking, what do you have against Christians? I mean, even back when we were—" he hesitated a moment "—sneaking around to see each other, you weren't interested in church or anything to do with it."

"I was raised in church." She turned to stare out the window, her gaze distant. "But I haven't been since I was a kid when we attended in Fredericksburg."

"I remember you telling me that everyone there was snooty."

"It was my grandparents' church, on Mama's side. They were total snobs. Even though Dad had money too, they hated that he moved her to Medina. So to appease them, Mama agreed to go to their church and send me to private school." She marked a check by one of the numbers she'd called and wrote a note out to the side.

"I remember your dad was into class and status like

them, but your mom was completely down-to-earth. Like you."

"Dad wasn't a snob. They both taught me that nobody is better than anyone else. But Dad was always worried someone would show interest in me because of money. Before Mama, he was engaged to Delia Rhinehart. Until he found out she only wanted his portfolio. After that, he was wary of anyone who didn't have wealth."

It all made so much sense now. Her dad hadn't looked down on him. He'd feared Rance was after Larae's money. Because he'd been there. If Rance had only come clean about his Remington family ties, maybe her dad would have treated him differently. But he'd been too proud to rely on his family name to smooth things over for him.

"It was Delia Rhinehart who made me want nothing to do with church."

"There were some Rhineharts in our school, weren't there?"

"Her son and daughters."

"I think I remember her from school events. She was always with that Chadwick woman."

"That's her. Delia was the biggest gossip, constantly spreading rumors or making stuff up. Back then, I decided if she was a Christian, I didn't want to be one." Her eyes glossy, she blew out a big breath and swallowed hard. "After Mama's accident, Delia started a rumor that Mama was out at midnight because she was seeing someone else."

He touched her shoulder. "I'm so sorry you had to go through that." She'd never talked about it before. He'd only known that her mom had been comatose after a drunk driver hit her. She died months later when Larae was fifteen. Right about a year before he'd met her.

"In truth, Mama went to the overnight pharmacy to get Dad some cough medicine because he was recovering from bronchitis. I don't think anyone believed Delia, but

Dad and I never stepped foot in that church again. Or any church, for that matter. We'd run into Delia every once in a while. She never changed. It was mostly because of her that I decided to leave for Dallas. So she'd never get the chance to make my baby seem—dirty."

One mean-spirited woman had single-handedly caused Larae's dad to assume Rance was a gold digger and helped to keep Jayda a secret from him. A deep dislike for a person he barely remembered bubbled up in him, but he couldn't allow those feelings to take root. He was far from perfect himself. And he had to get through to Larae.

"That's not how all Christians are. We're still human. Some don't quite get their act together."

"I prayed—" her voice quivered "—so hard for Mama to make a complete recovery." Her tone grew cold, hard. "Instead, she languished in a coma for six months before she died. I didn't understand, and it drove me farther away from God."

Give me the right words, Lord. "Death is part of life. But He wants to help you through the hard times, if you let Him."

"I know. I figured that out after Jayda came. I was lonely and scared. My landlord led me to Christ and invited me to church." Larae stiffened and swiveled her chair from his comforting hand on her shoulder. Then she stood and stepped over to the printer. "So I am a Christian, but church just isn't my thing. I can find crude, catty, snobby people anywhere, so why bother with church? I can read my Bible and pray anywhere."

It was after Rance lost Larae that he went searching for something. Anything to help him move on. But he couldn't tell her that. Not without getting into why he'd broken up with her. Not without putting a permanent smudge on her father's memory for her. Even though he understood her father's actions better now, the truth would still hurt Larae. And he'd hurt her enough.

He cleared his throat. "After we broke up and you left, I realized I didn't want to be a playboy. I went to church with my folks, which I'd done the entire time I was growing up. This time, I really listened. And it all sank in. I realized I was a sinner who needed a Savior."

"I'm glad. I don't know how I made it through Mama's death without Him." She set several flyers in the paper cutter and began making precise slices between each number tab.

"The people at our church are really down-to-earth and supportive. I'm confident you'd like it there."

"I haven't stepped foot in Medina for almost eight years. I'm about to show up with a daughter in tow and no husband. And run around town with you hanging flyers." She closed her eyes. "People might suspect who Jayda's dad is. I'm not ready for that to be public knowledge. I mean— she doesn't even know yet. I don't need a bunch of church tongues wagging, too."

"My church isn't like that, and no one in town will suspect anything. Jayda's small for her age. I didn't figure it out until she told me how old she was."

"I told her not to go around announcing her age to strangers. It's spring break right now." She finished slicing and set the stack of flyers on the desk. "If we stay here, I'll have to get her into school, and then everyone will know how old she is. The guessing games will begin on who her father is. I know how small towns are."

"Eventually, it's gonna be public news, Larae. You may as well prepare for it. But for now, we're working on a rodeo together and we went to the same school. Remember, we were very discreet back in the day when we were keeping your father in the dark." Her dad never would have known if he hadn't followed Larae when she'd slipped out to meet him one night. "Trust me, no one at my church will concern themselves with your marital status or single mom-hood. They'll just love you."

"I guess as long as you don't make I'm-your-dad eyes at Jayda, no one will suspect."

"I'll try real hard not to do that." He grinned. "And once Jayda knows about me and we're ready to go public with our little family, I'm certain the church will support us."

"Mama." Jayda stepped through the doorway. "Are we going to church?"

"I don't think so, sweetie."

"My friend Gretchen always goes to church. She makes it sound really fun." The wistfulness in Jayda's tone tugged at her.

The printer spit out the last copy. Larae scooped up the final stack and made the cuts. "Are you ready to go?"

"Can I hang flyers?" Jayda did a little bounce, successfully distracted from the church subject.

For now. But maybe he could use her curiosity to get Larae to try it out.

"I'm counting on it." Larae handed the little girl the tape dispenser.

Rance grabbed the stack of flyers. He'd have to tread carefully. She'd been hurt by a churchwoman, who obviously hadn't lived according to biblical values. He had to find a way to show her most Christians were loving and supportive. Her relationship with God would never fully progress if she ignored the Bible's instructions on assembling with other believers.

For now, though, he needed to focus on spending the day with his daughter—without letting her know he was her daddy.

Chapter Six

They'd ended up having to complete their task this morning in order for Rance to make church last night. And despite Jayda's pleas, Larae had refused to go to the service with him. Her little girl hadn't argued much. The trek had worn her out, and she'd slept soundly last night.

Thankfully, day two of being cooped up in a truck with Rance and watching him bond with their daughter was about to end.

"Last stop, the Apple Store," Rance announced.

"Are we gonna buy a computer?" Jayda sat up straighter in her car seat to peer out the windshield.

"You've never been here?" Rance hung his head. "Your mama should be ashamed. Can you eat a computer?"

"No, silly." Jayda giggled.

"Well, everything here is edible and made from apples. Because Medina is the Apple Capital of Texas."

As he turned into the only open slot in front of the rock building with red trim, memories flooded Larae. Of coming here with Mama. Buying fresh apple-pumpkin nut bread, sugar-coated pecans and apple-peach cobbler jam. But mostly the grip of Mama's soft, gentle hand until Larae learned not to touch anything. The sound of her laughter. The smell of Mama's apple shampoo and body splash. Larae wore both now, but somehow neither smelled as good as they had on Mama.

"Are we going in, Mama?"

Larae snapped to attention. Jayda was looking at her with rounded eyes in the rearview mirror. Rance's hand rested on his door, and he was watching her.

"Sorry. I used to come here with your grandma. Got lost in some good memories for a minute."

"I can put the flyer up here, if you'd rather not go in," Rance offered.

"No. I'm fine. Jayda will love it here." She checked her watch. "And it's past time for lunch. We could grab a bite while we're here."

"Sounds good to me." Rance opened his door.

Larae climbed down from the ridiculously lifted pickup. At least there was a step rail, but she should have insisted on driving her SUV. She helped Jayda down, then held her hand as they walked along the sidewalk.

Larae could feel Mama all around her. She'd shared memories with Jayda but never taken her places she'd been with Mama, since they were mostly in Medina.

"Do they sell apples here?"

"Even better. They grow them in the orchard. Along with several other fruits. And pumpkins. You can pick them yourself. Or at least, that's how it used to be."

"I wanna pick apples, Mama. And pumpkins."

Larae laughed. "We'll see if there's anything to pick and come back another day for sure."

"I must admit—" Rance ducked his head "—I've forgotten everything I used to know about picking seasons. Actually, I think I blotted it from my memory. I picked it all growing up, and when it's hot all day it's not so much fun."

"I've never picked anything." She hated to admit another glaring contrast between them as they strolled the sidewalk, lined with potted apple trees for sale. "They make their own honey, too. The honeybees used to get inside the café sometimes, so if that happens and one comes near you, just be still until they move on and they won't bother you."

They stepped inside. Several shoppers browsed the gift shop, but there was no line. Larae hurried to the register.

"May I help you?" a clerk with a sweet smile asked.

"Do you have somewhere we can hang this?"

"Sure. Ooh, my nephew will be excited." The woman rolled her eyes. "He rides bulls—for some reason. Let's put it on the bulletin board." She gestured behind them.

Larae turned to see a completely full corkboard.

"Oh, dear." The clerk came out from behind the counter. "I try to keep this cleaned off, but it gets away from me sometimes." She pulled a flyer announcing a barbecue. "See, this has already passed."

"Can I hang it?" Jayda asked.

"Sure, I'll give you a boost."

"Here, let me help." Rance knelt on one knee beside Jayda. "You can use my leg as a step."

Jayda giggled. "Okay."

Rance offered his hand and helped her up.

And seemed to promptly melt at the touch of his daughter's small fingers. His green eyes went all soft and warm. He couldn't put on an act like that, could he? Had he really changed?

But even standing on Rance's knee, Jayda couldn't quite reach the empty spot on the board.

"Is it okay if I lift you up?" Rance asked, but he turned to Larae for her permission, as well.

"Yes, please." Jayda stretched for all she was worth, with her tongue stuck out in concentration.

Rance waited for Larae's nod before he gently lifted the child.

"Let me do the tack." Larae grabbed an empty one from the board and pinned the flyer in place.

"That's perfect." Rance set his daughter down. Clearly

dazed to his core by the close encounter, he swallowed hard. "Let's go eat."

Larae reclaimed Jayda's hand in case he got any ideas.

"Can we look at all the pretty things first?" Jayda tugged toward a display of wind chimes.

"Tell you what, let's go look at the menu." Rance motioned toward the back of the store. "Figure out what you want, and I'll order it while y'all shop."

Like a dutiful father. And husband. What was going on here? Who was this guy?

"Okay."

He led them to the back, and they stepped down to the indoor patio.

"Larae Collins, is that you?" A woman seated between two children waved from a table.

"Stacia Keyes. Wow."

"Look at us, both in domestic bliss." Stacia wiped at something on her blouse with a napkin, then stood to hug Larae.

"It's so good to see you." Larae teared up as memories of Stacia's mom and Mama visiting back and forth over the years flooded over her. Playing Barbies and giggling about boys while their moms caught up. They hadn't seen each other since Stacia's sister died a few years ago, when Larae had left Jayda with Lexie and come for the service in San Marcos. "How's your dad?"

"He's getting his tea refilled," Stacia said.

She turned to see Maverick smile and wave from the counter.

"I was so sorry to hear about your dad." Stacia took both her hands. "I couldn't come to the service because the twins were sick."

"I know, your dad told me. It's okay."

Stacia let go and knelt in front of Jayda. "Aren't you a pretty little thing?" She turned to her twin niece and nephew. "This is Madison and Mason. Say hi, kids."

"Hi," the two echoed.

"I'm Jayda."

"My daughter," Larae clarified.

"I had no idea. We should get together sometime and let the kids play. And we could catch up, like our moms used to."

"I'd love that." With the twins probably around five now, Stacia likely assumed Jayda wasn't much older. But Jayda had always been good with younger children.

"Hi, Rance. I didn't mean to ignore you." Stacia's gaze cut back and forth between them, obviously wondering what they were doing together. "It's just been a long time since I've seen Larae. And I see you at church all the time."

"No worries."

"I may end up staying here." Larae rushed to derail anything Stacia might assume about them. "I'm starting a rodeo. I've hired Rance as my stock contractor, and since he's my only employee so far, he's helping me put up flyers about it around town."

"That sounds fun. And like something this town needs. I hope it comes together for you."

"Me, too." Sort of. If only everything about Rance wasn't so worrisome—that he might get tired of playing dad, take off for the rodeo circuit again, let Jayda down.

Mason giggled as he splatted his palm in a puddle of catsup, splashing his sister, who let out a squeal.

"Oh, dear." Stacia grabbed several napkins. "The kids are getting restless. I'm afraid we'll have to hurry. But call me at the store and we'll set something up. I mean it."

"I will. I promise."

"How's my second favorite girl?" Maverick set down his disposable cup to hug her.

"Doing well. It's good seeing you."

"Okay, Dad," Stacia said. "This one needs an attitude

adjustment for shooting that one with catsup, so we need to go. But Larae's coming to see us real soon. Right?"

"Right."

"I'm holding you to it."

"Mama, I want a grilled cheese. Can I go look at those sunflowers?" Jayda said.

"As long as you don't touch them. They're not real, just for decoration, and we don't want to mess up the pretty display."

"Yes, ma'am."

They placed their orders, then chose a table.

"So how do you know Stacia?" Rance asked.

"Our moms were best friends since childhood. They visited a lot, so Stacia and her sister, Callista, were always at our house or I was there." Larae slid onto a picnic table bench. "I was always closer to Stacia than her younger sister. Their mom died of a heart attack a few years before we lost Mama." Just saying the words put an emptiness in her stomach. "Stacia was a pillar of strength, but Callista took it really hard."

Stacia had helped her greatly through her mother's death. If not for her, Stella and Lexie, Larae would have pulled the covers over her head and stayed in bed. "I went to Callista's funeral a few years ago in San Marcos, but I haven't seen Stacia since then."

"I remember Callista from church when we were kids. I don't think she ever came after their mom died. I can't imagine losing my mom, especially at a young age. It makes me want to call her, right now," Rance said.

"Better yet, once we get home, you should go visit her."

"Good idea." He sighed. "To be honest, I've avoided them since finding out about Jayda. I can't tell them yet, and I hate keeping things from them."

"I'm sorry. I hadn't thought about them in my grand scheme of taking time."

"It's okay. For now." His gaze went to Jayda. "I'll tell

them I have a surprise coming for them, but I can't tell them what it is yet. Their anniversary is coming up, so that'll keep Mom from knowing I'm hiding something."

Larae blew out a breath and tilted her head toward Jayda. "She likes you. That's a start. It'll make things easier."

Except that there was nothing easy about this situation. Especially not for her heart. Because spending days like this with Rance made her remember why she'd fallen in love with him in the first place.

How had it come to this? Ringing the bell on door of his daughter's home. He should be married to her mother, living in the same house. Should have seen her born, raised her up to this point. Instead, Rance rang the bell like a guest. Heaviness landed in his chest again.

The door swung open to reveal a harried Larae on the phone, her hair in a messy ponytail. She held one finger up, then hurried back to the office. He considered having a seat in the living room, then followed her.

The smell of markers hung thick in the office. Large poster boards lined the wall at the end of the conference table. Larae's careful black print listed all the positions she needed to fill for the rodeo. Penciled in were over a dozen names and numbers.

"Yes, of course, Mr. Oliver. I've got your number and as soon as I have a solid grand opening date, I'll give you a call with more details and a timeline. Yes. Thank you for calling." She ended the call. "That was a professional bullfighter. He's been working in Houston but would like a steady year-round job closer to home. I've been inundated with calls about the rodeo all morning."

"I can see that."

"They started last night, and it's been like this all day."

"I think you've got yourself a rodeo."

"Yes, if it keeps on like this. I've had someone on both

lines several times, so as soon as I answer one call, there's another on deck."

"You have two lines here?"

She pointed to the ancient rotary phone sitting on the end of the table. "We still have the landline, so I listed it on half the flyers and my cell on the other half."

"I can man the second phone. If I can remember how to use one of these, that is."

"It's okay, I can handle them both."

The wireless she held pealed just as the rotary rang.

"Or maybe not." He picked up the rotary. "Collins Ranch, may I help you?"

"Heard something about y'all starting a rodeo," said the caller.

"Yes, sir. Are you interested?"

"I used to be a timer in Mesquite, but my wife's job transferred her to San Antonio. Since then, I've traveled around and worked several rodeos in the area. I'd love a steady job in one place."

"Well, we don't have a definite grand opening date just yet." Rance looked at the slots next to *Timer* on the poster board. Both empty. "If you'll give me your name and number, I'll let you know in a few weeks." He almost crashed into Larae head-on as she shifted to the other side of the board to write.

He took the name and number, but before he could share the news with her, the landline rang again. They spent the next several minutes answering calls, writing names and numbers, and crossing paths back and forth.

Five calls later, he hung up and realized she wasn't on the phone, either. But she was tangled in his phone line with the coils around one shoulder and her tiny waist.

"Oops. I forgot about the cord."

"I can tell." She tapped the pointy toe of her cowboy boot.

He lifted the receiver over her shoulder, then reached

on each side of her waist to unwind it from behind her back. Too close. Why hadn't he simply walked a circle around her? Too late now.

"I'll do it." Obviously uncomfortable with their proximity, she took a step back.

The receiver slipped from his hand and tangled even more behind her back.

"Just stay still." He circled behind her, fiddled with clumsy fingers at the coiled knot at the back of her waist.

"Just cut it."

Did he imagine her sharp intake of breath at the brush of his fingers? Or was it his gasp?

"It's a perfectly good phone. Might even be an antique. And this number is on half the flyers. Just be still, I've almost got it."

He got the final twist out to free her, stepped in front of her, unwound the length of cord and set the receiver in place.

"I'm investing in a wireless. Actually, I might even get rid of the landline."

"If you're gonna have a rodeo, you should keep it." He should take a step back, but the softness in her pale blue eyes drew him in.

"I guess that's true."

His gaze dropped to her lips.

"Mommy, are we gonna hang flyers again today?"

They sprang back from each other as if they'd been caught.

Jayda stood in the doorway. "What are y'all doing?"

"Nothing, Pumpkin." But Larae's face went scarlet. "Just talking about the rodeo. Look at all the calls we got today from people interested in it."

Had she wanted to kiss him, too? "I think we already hung all the flyers we needed to." Rance held his hand up for Jayda to high-five. "Good job."

Her tiny hand smacked his. "So since you're not doing

anything, can you come watch me ride, Mommy? You too, Rance?"

"Sure." Their voices blended, and Larae shot him a glare, as if she'd wanted him to decline.

They were so gonna have to talk about this.

"Yay." Jayda clapped her hands.

"But you'll have to ride in the barnyard for the next several weeks since they're starting to work on the arena today."

"Come on." She turned and skipped down the hall.

Larae started to follow, but Rance gently caught her arm. "What?" she said.

"We need to talk."

"Right now, I'm watching my little girl ride. Everything else can wait." She gave him a pointed look, then strode down the hall.

But she couldn't avoid him forever. He followed her out the back door.

They paused to watch the crew busily upgrade the arena railing, and by the time they reached the barnyard Jayda was astride the pony. The pinto's creamy mane and tale flounced as she trotted.

"See how good I ride, Rance? I've been riding all by myself for years."

"You're perfect." Jayda absolutely mesmerized him. He could watch her all day. But he was on the outside looking in. And he wanted more—much more—with his daughter.

And maybe even with Larae.

Chapter Seven

"So how's the rodeo coming?" Denny leaned against the porch rail, casting a long shadow over her list. "Stella said the phone's been ringing off the hook since yesterday. Did you get enough interest?"

"I checked references and, with your input on candidates, I actually have all the staff I need. And enough competitors to get started." The porch swing she sat on crept slowly back and forth. Kind of how she felt about the rodeo—not sure which way to go. "But should I really do this?"

"Sounds to me like this thing's coming together. And you've already started construction."

"I know. But should I really take what's left of the ranch account and sink it into something that might fail? The cost of the outdoor arena improvements, a concession stand, bathrooms, bleachers, the indoor building, and staffing—it's exorbitant."

"Well, once the indoor building is complete, you could rent the outdoor arena to competitors for practice."

"That's a good idea."

"The concession stand will bring in revenue."

"I'm afraid I'll need more than that. Especially since my rodeo won't serve alcohol."

"You could board horses for regular competitors."

Rance climbed the porch steps. "That way they wouldn't have to haul them around every weekend."

Where had he come from? She hadn't noticed him approaching around the side of the house. Always sneaking up on her. Why couldn't he stay out of her hair? Still, he had a point.

"That could work." She tapped her chin with a forefinger as inspiration struck. "A horse camp with campgrounds for tents and RV hookups so the competitors can stay for the weekend. Some might even want to permanently rent space for the RVs and horse trailers with living quarters."

"Now you're thinking like a marketing guru." Rance settled on the swing beside her.

Invading her space. As usual. Her pulse kicked up. As usual.

"I can see it now." Rance pointed past the barn. "That wooded area next to the south pasture would be perfect for campgrounds and RVs."

Exactly where she'd been thinking. She'd spent entirely too much time with him lately. Now they were thinking alike.

"How can you not be sure about the rodeo?" He tapped the list in her lap. "Looks like your staff's taken care of, with a few spares. And there are enough competitors to get this show on the road."

"But what if I use all the ranch capital we have left and fail?"

"You don't sink everything you've got into it. You get a business loan. How do you think I started my business?"

"Go into debt?"

"He's got a point." Denny adjusted his hat. "If you fail, you've got the ranch capital to pay off the loan. Then you sell the ranch for a reduced price like you planned to do when you first came here. But you gave saving this place your best shot. And I don't know of any rodeo failing. We're in Texas."

"And don't forget sponsors." Rance took his hat off, set it in his lap and finger combed his short-cropped hair. He still had hat ring. "Companies hang their signs in your arena—for a price. That'll help with overhead, too."

Why hadn't she thought of that? She'd been in charge of rounding up sponsors at her job in Dallas. She knew all the right people. But using her own money, risking the ranch where she'd grown up, taking out a business loan—it was scary stuff. And having Rance so close froze her brain.

"Since Rance here only raises bulls, broncs and steers, we could get into raising horses for barrel racing. And Larae was quite the barrel racer not so long ago. You could charge for lessons."

"You could raise roping horses, too." Rance snapped his fingers. "Denny was quite the steer header if I remember right. He could teach roping."

"My rodeo won't have calf roping. I know they say it doesn't hurt those poor little calves, but getting thrown down can't feel good. Same goes for steer wrestling. Only team and breakaway roping."

"Sounds like you've made up your mind, Miss Definitely My Rodeo." Rance grinned.

"It's your decision." Denny shifted his weight. "If you want to play it safe, go back to plan A, I still have that buyer's number."

"No." Not only would she lose the ranch, Denny and Stella. All the hands would be without jobs. She knew what that felt like. But she had an inheritance to fall back on. "I think we should do this. It's my only chance to save the ranch."

"For what it's worth, I think you're doing the right thing." Denny tipped his hat and loped off the porch. "Let me know what I can do to help."

"You could be my announcer."

"Well, now." Denny turned back to face her. "It's been a few moons since I've done that."

"Just like riding a bike. All you have to do is get back in the saddle."

"I'll think on it." He ambled toward the barn.

And suddenly she was alone with Rance.

Until the door opened and Jayda popped out.

"Hey, Mommy. Hey, Rance. Denny said I could ride Beans this morning." She plopped into Larae's lap.

"Just don't ride too long. Mr. Denny has work to do, and we don't want him to get behind."

"I won't, Mommy. Can we go with Rance to church tomorrow since we didn't get to the other night?"

"Of course you can," Rance answered before she could come up with an excuse.

Larae shot a glare at him, but his gaze was riveted on Jayda.

"Thanks, Rance." Jayda turned to give Larae a hug, hopped off her lap and started toward the steps. But she stopped, whirled around and opened her arms toward Rance. "Mommy says we're huggers. Do you like hugs, Rance?"

Larae's breath smothered in her chest as Rance leaned forward and her little girl's arms wrapped around his neck.

"I sure do. Especially from the prettiest little filly in Texas." His words came out thick.

"Why, thank you, kind sir." Jayda pulled away from him and curtsied. "Mommy says we always thank people for compliments and watch our manners."

"Your mama's right about that." His green eyes were all misty, and his throat convulsed with his effort to keep it together.

She was having the same problem, for different reasons.

Thankfully, Jayda didn't seem to notice. She clambered down the steps and skipped toward the barnyard.

"You had no right to answer her about church, and I have no intention of going."

"You don't have to. I can take her."

"You most certainly will not."

His gaze turned sheepish. "I'm afraid I have a hard time telling her no. Just come once. Then if you don't like it, maybe you'll at least feel comfortable with letting her go with me."

"I have calls to make." She stopped the swing, intent on escaping him. And church.

He caught her wrist. "I'll help you make them. But first, when do you plan to tell her?"

"Soon."

"How soon is soon?"

"Soon."

"What's holding you back?"

Her insides stilled. "I don't want to introduce you into her life if you're not planning on being a permanent fixture."

"That's exactly what I'm trying to be."

"But what about when your business is up and running? Will you go back to the circuit, then?"

"I'm officially retired. For good. After my last rodeo injury, I ended up with a shoulder replacement. That's why I started my business. Now I don't want to be Rance to her. I want to be her father."

"And you will."

"Tonight. I want you to tell her tonight." The uncompromising steel in his tone sent chills over her.

He was setting the deadline to open her daughter's heart up to him. Locking him into their lives. For as long as he felt like sticking around, anyway.

"Please, Larae. Tell her tonight." The catch in his voice tugged at her.

"Tonight it is."

* * *

Boards creaked and groaned with each step as Rance paced the old house. What was going on next door? Did Jayda know about him yet? Would Larae call once she'd broken the news?

The place needed some sprucing up. If he was gonna be a daddy to Jayda, the house needed to look and feel like a home. He hadn't done anything other than move furniture in. It was too stark, with bare walls. Maybe some plants or throw pillows. He'd ask his mom to help.

It wasn't dark yet. Larae had had plenty of time. Maybe he should just go on over there.

He bolted for the door, out the side gate, down her long driveway and then loped up onto her porch. Larae would be madder than a red wasp drunk on fermented plums over him just showing up. But Jayda was his, too, and it was high time he got to claim her. He rang the bell.

Several seconds ticked past before the door swung open. Larae's brows shot into a V. "What are you doing here?"

"Have you told her yet?"

"I'm working on it."

"How about we work on it together?"

"No. We're about to eat supper, and I'm doing this my way."

He crossed his arms under his chest. "We're both her parents—maybe we should start trying *our* way."

"So you came to bully me with your bulging biceps."

"No." His hands dropped to his sides. "Of course not. Come on, Larae, work with me here. You've had her for seven years. It's my turn."

"You have no idea how hard this is." Her chin trembled. "Explaining to her that she has a father. And I kept you from her." Her eyes went all glossy. "I didn't think you'd care."

His anger melted away. "Well, I do. But I'm not here

to fight with you. I just want her to know the truth. How about we tell her together and not point any fingers or blame?"

"I don't know."

"I didn't know Rance was coming to eat supper with us." Jayda bounced around Larae. "We're making dessert." She grabbed his hand. "Come on. You can help. Mommy makes the best roast in the whole world."

"The whole world, huh?" Rance shot her a wink. "Sounds like something I need to get in on." He sidestepped Larae as Jayda tugged him inside.

"We're making million-dollar cake, and it's so much fun." Jayda didn't let go of him until they were in the kitchen. "And so yummy."

It was the farthest he'd ever been in the ranch house. The kitchen was warm and rustic with knotty pine cabinets and walls, and there was an adjoining great room with cowhide and leather furnishings. But he was much more interested in his daughter—and her mother—than his surroundings.

Storm clouds brewed in Larae's icy blue eyes. "I'll get the cake out of the oven. Jayda, go to the bathroom and wash up. You smell like a horse."

"I do." Jayda giggled. "Okay, but don't start without me." She wagged her finger at Rance.

"I won't 'cause you gotta tell me what to do."

Jayda scurried down the hall.

"You could have begged off." She slipped on an oven mitt and scooped the cake out, setting it on a metal cooling rack on the counter. "I never agreed to tell her with you here."

"She dragged me here. There's not much I could do."

"Oh, come on," Larae scoffed. "She's seven and tiny. And you've got biceps."

His grin tugged into place. "You seem to be obsessed with my biceps."

"I am not." She rolled her eyes. "Why don't you just leave while she's gone and let me do this?"

"What are you so afraid of, Larae?"

"If you must know." She tugged off the mitt and threw it on the counter. "That she'll hate me for not telling her about you for all these years."

"Well, for starters, she's not old enough to connect all that. Or for resentment to set in. Just brush over the facts and don't dwell on the secrets. I'll help you."

She straightened her shoulders and gave a quick nod, resolve settling in.

Jayda skipped back into the room. "Can Rance poke the holes in the cake, Mommy?"

"But that's your job sweetie."

"I know, but I want Rance to do it."

"If you're sure."

Jayda grabbed a red-and-white straw from a drawer and handed it to him. "You take this and poke holes all over the cake. But not too close together or it will get all messy looking. I like to keep them about an inch apart."

He sank the straw into the golden cake near the corner. "Like this?"

"Yep. Now pull it out and just keep poking."

The straw left a round hollow in the fluffy, buttery confection. It smelled like Twinkies. He poked another hole and another.

"That's it. You're doing it perfect."

Jayda's approval melted his insides. To the point of making him tear up. "I can make holes, but I can't bake a cake to make them in." He had to keep things light. For her sake.

"That part's easy. It comes in a box, and you just add stuff."

He shot Larae a grin, but she wasn't concerned that Jayda had ratted her out. That little line between her eyes was obviously about him.

"Now your straw will get full of cake, so I'll get you another." Jayda handed him a fresh straw. "It's just a yellow cake now, but we're fixin' to make it yummy."

He finished his last row of holes. "Is that enough?"

"Yep. Now we're gonna make it yummy." She loaded a small can on the electric opener. The appliance hummed while the can spun and then stopped.

"I'll get it." Larae tunneled between them and removed the can and lid. "Jayda's not allowed to touch once it's open in case there are sharp edges." She set the can in his hand and slipped away behind them.

The brush of her fingers sent warmth through him.

"Now pour that on the cake." Jayda instructed.

"What is it?" The yellow thick liquid reminded him of spun honey.

"This is the yummy."

"It's sweetened condensed milk," Larae supplied. "Basically thickened milk and sugar."

"It sounds like the yummy." He poured the goo over the cake. It puddled and sank into some holes.

"Now you have to take this and spread it all over." Jayda handed him a large spoon. "While you do that, I'll open the pineapples."

"You mean there's more?" The sweet milk soaked into the cake.

"Lots more."

The hum of the opener started up, and once again Larae stepped between them to retrieve the can and lid. This time she set the crushed pineapple on the counter instead of in his hand.

Had his touch affected her, too?

"Now dump the pineapples on top and smooth them over like you did the yummy."

The juice soaked into the cake and ran into the holes he'd made while he spread the crushed fruit.

"You did good." Jayda took his spoon and licked

it clean. "By the time we eat, it'll be cool, and I'll put whipped cream and coconut on top."

"You know so much about cakes, I think you're gonna be a baker someday."

"No. I wanna be a princess."

"Well, there isn't any royalty in Texas. But you can be whatever you want to be."

Larae shot him the evil eye, probably longing to explain to her daughter that there were no princes. Only teenage bronc riders who broke hearts and moved on to the next girl.

He turned around as Larae took three large stoneware bowls and matching saucers out of the cabinet. "Let me get that." Another brush of their hands.

Did he imagine her sharp intake of breath?

"I don't know where y'all sit." He turned to the small pedestal table surrounded by four chairs. A pan of corn bread sat in the center.

"I'll set the table." Jayda brought silverware and napkins while Larae filled the glasses with ice. "Mommy sits here, 'cause she likes to look out the window, and I sit here. You can sit by Mommy so you don't block her view." She put the three settings in place.

"You're good at this."

"Thanks. I always set the table for us."

"I hope you still like sweet tea." Larae brought two glasses of amber liquid. "It's all we drink, so it's all I've got. Apart from milk or water."

"It's all I drink, too." He hurried to the counter to get the third glass for her. When he returned to the table, Larae was unlatching the lid of a robot-looking Crock-Pot with a digital display.

"I hope you like pork roast."

"I do, and it smells divine."

She scooped slabs of meat, thick fragrant gravy, and

potatoes and carrots into each bowl, while he used a spatula to serve the corn bread.

As soon as they sat down, Jayda and Larae dug right in.

Rance usually prayed before he ate, but he didn't want to make them uncomfortable. If eating together became a habit—and he hoped it would—he'd ease them into praying first. This time, he just said a quick silent prayer, thanking God for Jayda. And for bringing Larae back into his life.

His hand shook as he reached for his fork. Would Jayda be happy to know about him? Or would she see him as an intrusion into her one-parent world?

Chapter Eight

The roast was tender and flavored just right. But with Rance sitting next to her and the impending conversation hanging in the air, after a few forced bites, Larae couldn't eat. Nerves zinging, she pushed a carrot around with her fork while Jayda talked nonstop about how much more she liked the ranch, the kittens in the barn and riding Beans than their condo in Dallas.

"Mommy, you're not eating. Or watching the birds. Or talking like you normally do."

"I was just listening, Pumpkin. And I may have sampled a bit too much of the roast while it was cooking. I'm just not very hungry."

"How old is Beans, Mommy?"

"She's twenty-one, but ponies can live into their thirties. She still has lots of rides left in her, and the exercise is good for her."

"So why is Beans named Beans? It's not a very pretty name for a girl."

Larae chuckled. "She's a pinto pony. Pinto is a type of bean—the kind we call brown beans."

"Oh." Jayda giggled. "That's funny."

"Your grandma named her, and she had a good sense of humor."

"Your grandma was a very kind lady." Rance pushed his plate away. "And a good cook if she taught your mama how to make this. I think this is the best pork roast I've ever eaten."

"Thanks." But Larae's mood sank again with the reminder of his presence.

"I'm ready for dessert. Can we put the whipped cream on the cake yet, Mommy?"

"Let me feel the pan and see if it's cool enough." She stood, retrieved the cake and set it on counter, as Jayda scurried over to look.

Larae squelched a sigh as Rance stood and strolled over to Jayda's side like he belonged there. Jayda spread the whipped cream, then let Rance help sprinkle the coconut.

The only people who'd ever baked or eaten with them had been her dad, Lexie, an occasional friend from work and one of Jayda's school friends. Jayda didn't even know who Rance was yet, and he was infiltrating everything. Larae didn't like it. Not one bit.

"Do we need to let the cake chill a bit longer with the topping on it, Mommy?"

"Probably wouldn't hurt. We don't want the topping to melt." She snapped a plastic lid over the cake pan and set it back in the fridge.

"So now would be a good time for that talk?" Rance leaned against the counter. A challenge dwelled in the depths of his green eyes.

She couldn't put this off any longer. He wouldn't let her.

"I guess. Let's go in the living room."

"What talk?" Jayda's gaze went from one adult to the other.

"Come sit with me." Larae took her daughter's hand as they made their way to the front room. This was the only room that still had her mother's touch—pastel vintage with French provincial touches in sharp contrast to the rest of the ranch house's horse-and-barbed-wire decor with its cowhide furnishings.

She settled on her mother's flowered couch and snuggled Jayda beside her. Rance hesitated as she wished the floor would swallow him. Could he read her thoughts? He took a seat on the other side of Jayda. Invading their boundaries. But all boundaries were about to fall away.

"Do you remember when you were younger and you asked me how come your friend Chloe had a daddy and you didn't?"

"Uh-huh, and you said that some kids have daddies and some don't. I'm just one that doesn't."

"But you do," Rance interrupted.

"I do?"

Larae shot him the evil eye. "I'll handle this."

"I'm just trying to help."

"Who is my daddy?" Jayda looked back and forth between them.

"Rance is your daddy, sweetie."

"He is?" Her eyes grew huge as she turned to Rance.

"I'm sorry I haven't been around before now, Jayda." His eyes were misty.

"And I'm sorry I'm just now telling you this. But—"

"See, your mommy and I were high school sweethearts, but I broke up with her over something stupid. Because teenagers are stupid. Especially teenage boys."

Jayda snickered.

Something stupid—like another teenage girl.

"By the time your mommy found out about you, I was off riding the rodeo circuit, and she was in Dallas for college. We lost touch, so she didn't know where to find me to tell me about you. But I can promise you one thing, Baby Girl."

"What's that?" Jayda hung on his every word, obviously warming to him.

"If I'd known about you, I'd have been around. For every minute of your life."

Jayda turned to Larae and frowned. "So, were you and Rance married, Mommy?"

"No, sweetheart." Larae hung her head. "He was just my boyfriend."

"I been wanting to ask this for a long time. Aren't only married people supposed to have babies? That's what Chloe said when I told her I didn't have a daddy."

"Oh, sweetie." Larae gave her daughter a little squeeze.

"That is the way it's supposed to be." Rance's tone dripped with regret. "The way God wants it to be. But people don't always do things the way God wants them to. And you just meeting me is a perfect example of why only married people should have babies. If your Mommy and I had been married, I'd have known about you from the beginning."

"Do you wish you hadn't broken up with Mommy and married her instead?"

Rance caught her gaze. "I certainly do."

"Well, why don't y'all get married now?"

"Jayda!" Larae tried to silence the child.

"Your mommy and I are just getting to know each other again." Rance lowered his voice. "And I'll let you in on a little secret."

"What's that?" Jayda asked.

"I'm pretty sure your mommy's still mad at me for breaking up with her back in high school."

Jayda turned to Larae. "Are you, Mommy?"

Larae drew in a deep breath. "A little."

"Well, I'm not mad at you. I mean, I wish you'd married Mommy. But I like you, and I'm glad you're my daddy." Jayda reached toward Rance.

He enfolded the tiny child in his arms. "Me, too, Jayda. Me, too." He blinked away tears, focused on Larae. *Thank you*, he mouthed.

"Can we have cake now?"

"It should be ready. Let's go see."

"Can you do that and let us sit here a minute?" Rance asked. "I mean it's not every day I get to officially meet my Baby Girl."

"Sure." Larae managed to sound fine. "I'll bring the cake in here. Do you want milk or tea with it?"

"Milk." Rance and Jayda's answers blended as one.

"I'll be right back." She stood. Put one foot in front of the other. Noodle legs.

And so it began. Sharing her little girl with Rance. Why did she feel she was losing something? Her daughter? Or her heart? Maybe both.

Rance stepped onto Larae's porch the next morning and rang the bell, then impatiently tapped his boot, eager to see Jayda.

The door swung open to reveal Larae. Her smile turned upside down at the sight of him.

"You can't just barge in any time you feel like it. You need to call first."

"To see my own daughter?" Irony coated his tone. "The one you didn't tell about me until yesterday. And you probably never would have told me if she hadn't enlightened me on how old she is."

"You're the one who broke things off with me."

He hung his head, closed his eyes. "You're right. I'm sorry."

"She doesn't need to hear us arguing."

"We need to get along for her sake." He pushed his frustration down. "I'll call next time. Or maybe we can set up a schedule. But I did sort of do that. Y'all are supposed to go to church with me."

"Oh, I forgot all about that." Her hands went to her hair, but her eyes belied her words. "There's no way I can get ready fast enough."

"We've got an hour. I came early in case you tried to back out."

"I haven't even fixed Jayda's breakfast yet."

"I can do that. Go get ready."

"You? Cook?"

"I've lived on my own a long time. I have to eat. Go on. I got this."

"Maybe we should just try for next week." She grabbed the doorknob, obviously prepared to shut the door in his face.

"Daddy!"

Mush. His being turned to mush as Jayda rushed under Larae's elbow and hurled herself into him. No words would form as he pried her arms loose enough to allow him to kneel and hug her back. He could stay in this moment forever.

Then Jayda got fidgety and tugged away from him. "Look at the dress I'm wearing to church." Pink fluff with a poofy skirt. She twirled, and her skirt billowed even more. "Mommy told me to take it off 'cause we're not going. But I told her you promised and you'd be here."

Rance's gaze swung to Larae's.

"I didn't think you'd remember." She looked away.

"Well, let me just set you both straight right now. If I say I'm doing something, I do it. Especially where Jayda's concerned."

"I hope so," Larae mumbled.

"No hoping about it."

"Daddy, why are you crying?" Jayda's small fingers touched his cheek.

He hadn't even realized. He caught her tiny hand. "Happy tears, Baby Girl. I'm happy to be your daddy and that we both know it."

"Me, too. I'm happy to be your Baby Girl."

"Let's eat some breakfast while Mommy gets ready." He scooped her up and stood as she giggled.

"Actually, Jayda, why don't you run on into the kitchen and get a couple of skillets out? I need to talk to Rance a minute."

"Okay, Mommy."

Regretfully Rance set Jayda down. "I'll be there in a minute."

She scurried for the kitchen.

"What about your parents?"

"I told them I hoped you and Jayda are coming to church with me and for lunch at their house afterward. If you'll agree, I figure we can clue them in then."

"You committed us to lunch? Without asking me?"

"I said I hoped and if you agree. But it's high time they know the truth. I've kept it from them long enough."

"You've only known for a week, Rance. Less than a week."

"Seven years, Larae. Seven long years."

She propped her hands on her hips. "Well, maybe if you hadn't moved on to the next rich girl in line, I'd have told you about her."

"You got me there." But she could never know why. Why did he keep losing his temper, snapping at her at every turn, when he was just as much to blame for all of this? He had to put a leash on his frustration.

She rolled her eyes. "In the future, will you please ask before planning my day?"

"I will. So should I tell them lunch is on?"

"Yes."

"Now go get ready."

"Wait. What if Jayda announces to everyone at church that you're her daddy. Including your parents."

"I'll talk to her while I cook. Tell her it's a surprise for my parents for after church and no one else needs to know before they do. Is she good at keeping a secret? As good as her mother?" He shot her a wink.

Her gaze narrowed. "I thought we were trying to get along and not accuse each other."

"I was teasing." He let out a big breath. "I'll work on my humor."

"Jayda is a good secret keeper."

"Okay, I'll handle it. Go get ready. If you hurry, you might have time to eat breakfast, too."

She hesitated, obviously not wanting to leave him alone with Jayda.

"I'm her father. I won't do anything to hurt her. Ever. Stop worrying." He gripped her shoulders gently and turned her toward the stairs. "Now git."

She swung back to face him with a mixture of storm and fear in her eyes. "Just know, if you hurt her, I'll hurt you." She whirled away and stalked toward the stairs.

He believed her. All five foot three and maybe a hundred and ten pounds of her. In mama bear mode. And way too cute for her own good. Way too much for his Larae-fixated heart.

But he could only build a relationship with Jayda. Not Larae. He'd practically admitted to her yesterday that he was still pining for her by saying he wished he'd married her. In the future, he'd have to guard his heart better. And his words. Even though her dad was gone, no one else would ever accuse him of being after anyone's money ever again. Best to steer clear of Larae and her trust fund.

And she'd kept Jayda from him for seven years. Despite the circumstances, he resented the years he'd lost.

His focus could only be on Jayda. And the rodeo. If he could help Larae make the rodeo a success, maybe she'd stay in Medina. That would keep Jayda close.

Chapter Nine

Larae had never felt this self-conscious in her entire life. Walking into church with Rance and Jayda. Like a family. Her insides shook. Would people figure out her secret? Or just assume they were dating?

Long white pews with blue padded seats lined the navy carpet. White walls, bright lighting, frosted windows. A piano and a pulpit graced the stage.

Only smiles greeted them. Maybe a bit of curiosity in the eyes of those who shook her hand, introduced themselves and said they were glad she was here. But no suspicion or judgment.

"Larae." Stacia hurried over and gave her a hug. "I'm so glad you're here."

Instantly Larae felt less uneasy. "I can't even tell you how happy I am to see you."

"Come sit with us." Stacia motioned to where her dad, Maverick, sat with the twins. "I've managed to teach the twins to be still and quiet, but I can't seem to conquer the sticky. I can't promise you won't get something on you, just by being close to us."

"We'll see if Dad wants to move back a pew." Rance looked around for his dad.

"I'll save seats, just in case." Stacia gave Larae another hug before returning to her seat.

"It's so pretty, and everyone's so nice," Jayda whispered.

"No Delia Rhineharts here." Rance gave Larae a confident grin.

"Who?" Jayda frowned up at him.

"Nobody, sweetie." Larae patted her hand. "Just some lady I used to know."

"I'm not saying anybody here is perfect. We're all a bunch of sinners saved by grace. But they're good folks."

"What's a sinner? And what's grace?" Jayda scrunched her eyebrows together.

"A sinner is somebody who does something wrong." Rance explained.

"Like what?"

What if Rance believed differently than Larae did?

"Well, the Bible says to honor your father and mother. So when your mama tells you to go to bed and you argue with her, that's dishonoring her."

Jayda's eyes grew big. "I've done that. I guess I'm a sinner."

"We all are, Pumpkin. But Jesus can fix us. Remember what I told you."

"That Jesus died on the cross for our sins. But I didn't know what sin meant."

Larae closed her eyes. How could she have failed to explain that? "Oh, Pumpkin. If I ever tell you something and you don't understand, just tell me. Or ask questions. Okay?"

"Okay, Mommy. So how does Jesus fix us?"

"Tell Him you're a sinner, that you're sorry, and ask Him to save you." Larae worked at keeping it simple. "If you mean it from your heart, He'll forgive your sins."

"And I'll get to go to Heaven like Grandpa?" Jayda asked.

"A long time from now, when you get really old, you will."

"I don't wanna get old and all wrinkly." Jayda shook her head.

Rance chuckled. "Wrinkles are the mark of wisdom."

"What's that?"

"It means you're really smart," said a man from behind Larae.

She turned around to see Rance's dad.

"Good to see you, Larae." His tone was genuine, yet his smile was cautious. "Who's this little beauty?"

"I'm Jayda. I'm small for my age, but I can't tell you how old I am." Her gaze cut to Rance. "'Cuz it's a secret."

Obviously, Rance had covered all the bases.

Davis grinned, so much like his son. "Well, you must be an awfully good secret keeper."

"Oh, I am. Mommy says if we can't keep secrets, no one will ever trust us."

Or we keep secrets that shouldn't be kept. With the same result.

Jayda peered up at him. "What's your name?"

"I'm Davis Shepherd, Rance's dad."

"You're Da—I mean Rance's dad?" She did a little bounce. "I'm so excited."

"Well, I'm excited, too." Davis chuckled. "I don't think I've ever quite gotten a reaction like that."

"Jayda's been looking forward to lunch." Larae tried to cover. "She really likes your son."

"No, I don't, Mommy. I love him. He's my—" Jayda's mouth clamped shut.

"New neighbor," Rance supplied.

Davis's gaze narrowed.

The piano grew louder, and Rance checked his watch. "Almost time to start. We better sit down. Stacia and Larae are old friends. Mind if we move back a pew so they can sit together?"

"Of course not. I'll get my Bible." Davis strolled toward the row in front of Stacia and her dad.

Perfect timing. Jayda would have to be quiet until after church.

Fifth pew from the front on the left, Rance filed them in, seating Larae beside Stacia.

"Where's your mommy?" Jayda asked Rance.

"Tickling the ivories." Rance pointed to the stage.

"I don't know what that means." Jayda's eyebrows scrunched.

"Piano keys used to have ivory overlays," Rance clarified, his tone patient.

"Oh, so it means she's the piano player." Jayda bent sideways to see around the woman in front of them.

"Don't worry, you'll meet her after church."

A woman's hand squeezed Larae's shoulder. "I'm tickled to see y'all here."

She turned to smile at Stella and Denny sitting behind them.

The song ended, and a man approached the pulpit.

Larae daydreamed through a few announcements and an opening prayer, then mouthed the words to three congregational hymns. After all the years she hadn't attended church, she still knew the songs by heart.

Singing along, Jayda turned the page of the hymnal after the first verse. Rance flipped it back and pointed with his finger to where the next verse began under the first.

Up until now, Larae had been the one to teach Jayda new things. Her heart tugged.

The sermon started and the preacher held her attention, as if his message on church attendance was for her alone.

"Christians aren't perfect. No one to ever walk this earth was perfect. Except Jesus. So when people upset you or even seriously wrong you, especially another Christian, you can't let that keep you from church." The preacher flipped the pages of his Bible.

"Hebrews 10:24 and 25 instructs us on this. 'And

let us consider one another to provoke unto love and to good works: Not forsaking the assembling of ourselves together, as the manner of some is; but exhorting one another…'"

The preacher scanned the crowd. "Be kind to each other. But if a flawed Christian brother or sister says or does the wrong thing, pray for them and keep coming to church. You can't grow as a Christian or have the relationship God wants you to have with Him, if you don't attend church with like-minded believers."

He moved on to the members needing to be a tight church family, there for each other and following the golden rule. But Larae's brain stayed snagged. Since she'd quit going to church, she'd spent time reading her Bible and praying. She'd taught Jayda about God. But she hadn't really felt close to Him. Not in a long time. If she'd taken her daughter to church all these years, Jayda would have understood what sin was.

The piano started up again, jarring her from her thoughts. The preacher made his plea for sinners to come to the altar to get saved and for Christians to leave their cares there. Familiar strains of "Just as I Am" and a sea of voices joined together. As several people went to the altar, Jayda squeezed in front of her, Stacia and Maverick, out the end of the pew, and headed toward the front.

Larae's feet launched into motion and she caught up with her daughter, catching Jayda's hand.

"Tell that man I want to get saved, Mommy," Jayda announced loudly enough for the whole church to hear.

Murmurs of *aww* and *how sweet* echoed behind them as they made their way to the altar.

"I think he knows, sweetie," Larae whispered.

"The faith of a little child, folks." The preacher met them at the altar, a little misty-eyed. He knelt with them there and asked Jayda several questions, making sure she understood the decision she was making. Satisfied that she did, he led her through the sinner's prayer. Almost word for word what Larae had said as she'd accepted Jesus when Jayda was a baby.

Guilt welled within her. *I'm sorry, God, for abandoning Your church. I'm sorry for not being as close to You as I should have been. I want to do better, to get closer.*

"Amen," Jayda repeated after the pastor.

They all stood and the preacher moved on to someone else as Larae and Jayda returned to their seats.

Despite his smile, Rance had tears on his cheeks. She'd seen him show emotion twice now. Over Jayda. Had he finally grown up?

But no matter how appealing he was, no matter how caring—at heart, he was still a rodeo circuit junkie. He might try to settle down and stay put, but he might get a hankering for wild horses and leave again. Her job was to protect Jayda and comfort her daughter if he left. She couldn't take the chance of letting him break her heart, too. Not again.

Rance had ridden home with his parents. He'd given Larae instructions to drive his truck—slowly. He should have planned this better. Told his folks last night. But if he'd done that, they'd have immediately gone over to Larae's. And she was too gun-shy. She'd needed the night to adjust to Jayda knowing about him before his parents clamored for time with their grandchild.

Yet, this way, it all felt rushed. As soon as his dad pulled in the driveway, Rance jumped out.

"I have to tell y'all something."

"So tell us." Mom slipped her Bible in her large purse.

"Inside." He ushered them in.

"You're worrying me." His mom gave him a pointed inspection.

"Nothing to worry about, Mom. It's good news."

"Are you seeing Larae again?" She frowned. "She's

a sweet girl, but she hurt you once. And she has a child now. It's always so complicated when you take on another man's child. Is he involved in their lives?"

"I don't think there's another man, Maggie. I think Rance is trying to tell us that the little girl is his."

His mother's hand flew to her heart.

"How did you know?" Rance's gaze dropped to the hardwood floor.

"You mean it's true?" His mom sank into her rocking chair.

"The little girl, Jayda, was watching her words this morning, but I think she almost said you were her dad. And then when she went to the altar, I saw your reaction. I knew you hadn't known her long enough to love her like that. Unless she's yours."

"I'm sorry I didn't tell you." Why did he suddenly feel like a teenager who'd shamed his family? Because he had shamed their values. They just hadn't known until now. "But I just found out Tuesday. And Larae wanted time to tell Jayda about me and let her get used to that before grandparents flocked to see her."

"We have a granddaughter." His mother dabbed her eyes with tissue. "How could Larae keep her from us all these years?"

"Don't blame Larae, Mom. I broke up with her, and by the time she learned she was pregnant, I was dating someone else. And then another someone else. Larae thought I didn't care and was too immature to be a father, so she left for college without telling me. I can't say I blame her for the opinion she had of me."

"I don't understand." Mom frowned. "We always thought she broke your heart."

"The whole thing left me heartbroken, but I had a solid reason for ending things. I wouldn't have if I'd known about Jayda, though."

"You were just a kid, son." His father always had his back.

"But I knew better. You raised me to get married, then have kids. To follow God's leading, not my own."

"You're certainly not the first to have a child out of wedlock, son. And you won't be the last. Besides, you didn't ever decide to follow Jesus until after Larae."

"They'll be here soon. I know it's a lot, Mom." He strolled over to her side and put his hand on her shoulder. "But try to pull it together. You can't be mad at Larae. And if you blubber all over Jayda, it might freak her out."

She nodded, patted his hand and blew her nose. "I'll just focus on the good. I'm a grandmother."

The doorbell rang. "There they are. We cool?"

"As a key lime pie your mother won't let me have anymore."

"Oh, stop." His mother stood and hurried to get the door, as he and his dad followed.

Jayda stood on the porch, holding a sack. "I brought play clothes."

"Good." His mother opened the door wide. "I plan on doing lots of playing today."

"Do you know who I am?"

"We sure do." His father's voice was tight with the hold he had on his emotions.

"I'm Daddy's Baby Girl."

His mom's laugh came out watery. "That's a very fine name."

"And I like hugs," Jayda hinted.

"Good, 'cause we do, too." His father scooped her up into his arms, and his mother hugged them both.

His gaze went to Larae. She looked so lost, like she needed a hug. But that would be a very bad idea for his peace of mind.

"I'm really glad to have a grandma and grandpa, specially since my other grandpa went to Heaven."

"I imagine you miss him," his mother said. "But we're really glad to have a granddaughter. We've never had one before."

Someone's stomach growled from the hug huddle.

"Are you hungry, Jayda?" His mother withdrew a little.

"Mmm-hmm."

"Well, you came to the right place. I've got chicken in the Crock-Pot."

"I'll help you," Larae offered.

"Me, too," Jayda chimed in.

"How about you go change into your play clothes first?" his mom suggested. "That way you won't mess up your pretty dress."

"Okay."

"Come on." She clasped Jayda's hand. "I'll show you where the bathroom is."

That would leave his mom and Larae. Alone in the kitchen. Together. With seven years of secrets standing between them.

"Don't worry." His mother patted his arm. "We'll be fine."

So why did Larae kind of look like a sheep being led to the slaughter?

Hill Country Redemption 83

Chapter Ten

Larae should have stayed in the bathroom with Jayda. But her daughter had insisted she could change by herself and find the way to the kitchen.

"Rance has probably told you all about my low-fat cooking, but my mushroom gravy is to die for if I may say so myself." Maggie scooped heaping ladles of chicken and vegetables into a roasting pan. "You'll never miss all that fat and calories."

"He probably wouldn't have known the difference if you hadn't told him," Larae said. The pale yellow walls combined with white cabinets gave the space a bright, sunny appeal. But it did nothing to soothe Larae's nerves.

"The plates are in the cabinet to the left of the sink, silverware directly below and glasses on the right. If you'll set the table, I'll get the tea out."

"Sure." Larae found everything and went to work. Might as well address the elephant in the room head-on. "I'm sorry that you just now learned about Jayda."

"Rance explained everything. I'm afraid he was young, made some poor choices, and didn't treat you very well. I'm just glad I know now. And that you and Jayda are here today."

"I didn't consider you and Mr. Shepherd at all when I decided not to tell Rance about her."

"You were young." Maggie set the chicken on the table.

"And you were having to make some very adult decisions. Without a mother to guide you." She patted Larae's arm.

The tender gesture brought tears to Larae's eyes. She grabbed a glass and filled it from the ice dispenser in the refrigerator door, letting the clatter cover her emotions.

"I thought a lot of your mother," Maggie persisted. "It must have been tough losing her."

"It was." She filled the remaining glasses.

"I hope we can grow close." Maggie poured tea. "That you can come to count on me. No matter what happens between you and Rance."

"There's nothing between us. Not anymore. I mean—other than Jayda. He wants to be part of her life. But not mine."

"Still. I'd like us to be friends."

"I'd like that."

Maggie gave her quick hug, as Larae worked at blinking away the moisture.

Rance stepped through the entry, took one look at her and frowned at Maggie. "What did you say to her?"

"Nothing. I'm fine." Larae swiped at her eyes.

"Relax, Rance. I'm not a monster. Larae and I are bonding."

He caught Larae's gaze, questioning.

"She hugged me."

"Oh. Good. That's good."

Very good. Maggie was quite a woman. She had every right to be angry at Larae and to hold a grudge. Instead, she'd given a very much needed motherly hug.

"Is it time to eat yet?" Davis strolled into the kitchen holding Jayda's hand. "The princess's tummy won't stop growling."

"You must be growing." Rance knelt to Jayda's level. "I cooked you a good breakfast."

"Maybe I'm getting taller." Jayda giggled.

He stood. And realized both his parents were locked in on him with questioning eyes. "What?"

"You cooked Jayda breakfast?" Dad ventured.

Did they think he'd spent the night? His ears burned. "I stopped by to make sure they were coming to church with me. Jayda hadn't eaten yet, so I fixed breakfast while Larae got ready."

"Oh." Mom sounded relieved.

"I've grown a brain since I was eighteen, you know."

Larae's face went scarlet.

"I hope so, Daddy. Life would be hard without a brain."

A beat of silence and then they all laughed.

But the thing Larae noticed most was the way Rance's heart pooled in his green eyes every time Jayda called him Daddy.

As they gathered around the table, Larae thought back to her childhood, the last time she'd shared a meal as a family, back when her mom was alive.

Even if Rance hadn't really grown a brain. If he got bored playing daddy and ended up leaving, Maggie and Davis would be good for Jayda. She needed a family. And since Larae's father was gone, family was something she could no longer provide for Jayda. Maybe this would all work out. With or without Rance in the picture.

On monday morning, Larae pulled into the school parking lot. Medina had always been a close-knit small town, and most of the teachers at the public school used to go to Rance's church. Hopefully, it was still like that. She'd longed to go there when she was a kid instead of the private school where her parents had sent her.

Jayda hesitated, looking even smaller than usual and very uncertain.

"You ready?"

"It's smaller than my old school, and I don't know anybody here."

"I know, sweetie. But you'll make new friends."

"Okay."

Larae opened her SUV door and met Jayda on the sidewalk. A tiny hand slipped into hers. She hadn't been sure if Jayda would go all big girl on her or not. Apparently the insecure new girl needed her mother's reassurance. She squeezed Jayda's hand.

Why was starting somewhere new always so hard? It made her want to drop the whole rodeo thing and take Jayda back to her familiar school in Dallas with her friends.

A woman met them at the door with a smile. "Hello. Do we have a new student?"

"Are you starting school here?" a little girl asked.

"This is Jayda Collins, and today will be her first day."

"We saw y'all at church yesterday," the little girl said. "I'm Amelia Johnson, the hall monitor."

"And I'm Amelia's mother, Miss Marjorie. I'm the elementary secretary, manning the door this morning since the principal is in a meeting. What grade will you be in, Jayda?"

"Second." Jayda clung tighter to Larae's hand.

"I'm in second." Amelia did a little skip. "We'll be in the same class. And at church, too, if you come to Sunday school."

"Can I, Mommy?"

"Sure."

Relief warmed her worries. Her little girl would be fine. *Thank you, Lord, for Amelia and Marjorie.* "I'm Jayda's mom, Larae."

"Have you registered her yet?" Marjorie asked.

"No." Would Marjorie think her a bad parent for changing her daughter's school so near the end of the term? "I came here for spring break to sell my family ranch. But Jayda loves it here, so we decided to stay."

"I'll show you where our class is," Amelia offered.

Jayda let go of Larae's hand.

"We'll need to go to the office first. Which is exactly where I'm headed." Majorie checked her watch. "The bell will ring any minute. Amelia, you go on to your class. You'll see Jayda later. I expect you to keep an eye out for her and not let her get lost."

"I will, Mommy." Amelia waved as she turned the corner.

"Thank you." Larae pressed a hand to her heart. "That makes me feel better. Jayda, we need to check you in first, then you can go to class with Amelia."

"Okay, Mommy." She reclaimed Larae's hand.

"The office is right through here." Marjorie escorted them through the foyer lined with concrete block walls. "I know it's hard to leave our babies in a new place. But Jayda will be just fine. Amelia and I will see to it." Marjorie ushered them to seats and handed Larae a clipboard. "Once you get the top two sheets filled out, Jayda can go on to class while you finish."

Larae started on the paperwork while Jayda played a game on her phone.

"Can I go to class yet, Mommy?"

"Almost, Pumpkin." She finished the first sheet and started on the second.

Minutes passed as she listed Jayda's medical history and emergency contact numbers.

"I'm done." She stood to hand the two sheets to Marjorie at her desk.

"Yay, I get to go to class now."

"You sure do. I'll take you there while your mommy finishes up here."

"Give me a hug first." Larae opened her arms.

"Bye, Mommy." Jayda gave her a squeeze. "Don't worry. I already made a friend."

"I can't even tell you how glad I am to hear that." Larae kissed the top of Jayda's head.

Marjorie took Jayda's hand. "I'll be right back."

Jayda waved with a confident smile.

Larae almost burst into tears of relief. She worked at pulling herself together, moving on to the next page. Bus or pickup? Definitely not the bus. Larae didn't want Jayda exposed to older kids for an hour each morning and afternoon. She circled pickup, then listed her name and number and relation to Jayda.

Three more lines for authorized pickup names. She listed Denny and Stella as family friends, then wrote Davis and Maggie but hesitated over their relation. Rance was Jayda's father, and she might as well get used to it. She wrote in "grandparents," then listed Rance with his number as "father."

By the time, Marjorie came back, Larae was almost finished.

"Thank you for making this so much easier than I was expecting."

"I'm glad to help."

A few minutes later, Larae handed over the clipboard.

"Pickup." Marjorie explained where the pickup line entered and exited, then scanned the list. She didn't show any shock at Jayda's family ties. "Anyone other than you will have to provide identification, and Jayda will have to know them before we'll let her leave. But I actually know everyone on your list."

"That sounds good. You can never be too careful in this day and age."

"It's never been a problem around here, though." Marjorie smiled. "Okay, I've sent an email to her last school, so I should have her records in the next few days. We're all set."

"Thank you so much."

"I'll see you Wednesday night? At church."

"Yes, we plan on coming." Larae waved as she left the office and retraced her steps to the exit.

Outside, as she approached her SUV, she spotted Rance's truck. He got out and met her.

"What are you doing here?"

"I wanted to make sure everything went okay. Was she nervous?"

"At first. Until we ran into Amelia and Marjorie Johnson."

"They're good folk. Go to my church."

"Yes. Amelia remembered seeing us Sunday, and before I knew it, Jayda was champing at the bit to go to class with her new friend."

"I'm glad." He released a big breath. "I was worried about her. Changing schools can be tough on kids."

"You should probably stop lurking around or they might call Security."

"You're right. Except that Marjorie knows I'm harmless. How about we swing by the Old Spanish Trail for breakfast?"

"I can't. The arena guys are finishing up today."

"Anything I can help with?" Rance asked.

"I think it's all under control."

"I'll want to check on Jayda after school. Is it all right if I stop by later?"

"Of course."

"See you then." He sauntered to his truck, climbed in and drove off.

Now why was her heart all out of rhythm from spending two minutes with him?

Chapter Eleven

In the distance, Larae stood at the fence with her look-alike child. The afternoon sun shone in their spun-gold hair. So similar. Rance strolled up the driveway as several cowboys reinforced sections of the arena.

"Daddy!" Jayda whirled around and hurled herself into him.

She might look just like Larae, but she was Rance's, too. He scooped her up and swung her around as she giggled. When he set her down, he caught Larae's evil eye.

"What?" He splayed his hands palms up.

She made a slight motion with her head toward the ranch hands and arena crew.

The arena crew paid them no mind, but Denny and the hands were downright staring. Then they saw him returning the stare and all went back to work. Denny would hold his tongue, but the rest of them wouldn't. Soon all of Medina would know the secret that Larae had kept so carefully for so many years.

"Isn't it exciting? We're getting our own rodeo." Jayda clambered up the fence to the second rail and propped her elbows over the top.

"It is exciting."

"They're gonna break ground on the indoor arena soon. Mommy said that means dig in the dirt."

"That pretty much sums it up. How was your first day of school?"

"It was awesome. Amelia Johnson is my new bestest friend."

"Do you have any homework?" Larae asked.

"Nope. I got it done during last period when the teacher gave us quiet time."

Gravel crunched behind them, and Rance turned to see his parents' car pulling up to the house. Larae would probably kill him before the day was over. First he'd outed her to her employees, and now his parents were descending on her.

"I'll tell them it's not a good time." He started for their car.

"No. It's okay." Larae sounded like she meant it. "They're welcome anytime."

As his parents stepped from their car, Jayda realized who it was and launched toward them. "Grandma and Grandpa!"

"You sure about this?" He quirked an eyebrow at Larae.

"She needs family. And I don't have any secrets. Not here at least."

"Look, I'm really sorry about that. I didn't anticipate Jayda's reaction."

"At least this way I don't have to explain anything." She rolled her eyes.

His parents strolled over, each holding fishing poles, with Jayda in the middle latched onto their free hands.

"I hope it's all right for us to come." His mom smiled. "We probably should have checked with you first, but Jayda invited us to go fishing today."

"Grandma gave me her phone number, and I called to make sure it worked while you were cooking supper last night."

"It's fine." Yet strain showed on Larae's face. "Just

maybe let me know what's going on next time. And you're not supposed to make calls without asking me first."

"We can make it another time," his father hedged.

"Please stay. Jayda's been wanting to go fishing since we've been here, but I've been so busy."

Ah. It was guilt. "Why don't we all go?" Rance suggested.

"I'd love to, but the arena guys are here."

"They know what they're doing. You'll still be on the property, and they can call if they have questions."

"Come on, Mommy. Please."

Larae visibly caved. "Okay. Let's go." She turned to Denny. "Are the poles and gear still in the shed?"

"They are. There's a fridge full of bait and all the lures you can imagine. Your daddy did love to fish."

"Yes, he did." Larae went all soft with memories and teared up a little.

Uh-oh. Had she not wanted to go because she hadn't ever been without her dad? Or maybe because that had been their long-ago meeting spot where they'd shared lots of stolen kisses?

"Jayda, do you know where the river is?" Rance asked.

"Mommy took me there our first day here." She gave an adamant shake of her head. "But I can never, ever, ever go near it by myself."

"That's a very good rule. Since Grandma and Grandpa are with you, though, you could take them on down to the river while I get the gear, and your mama can finish up here."

"I can do that."

"I thought we were just fishing in some pond." His dad adjusted the brim of his floppy fishing hat.

"There's a narrow branch of river that runs across the ranch," Larae explained. "Pretty good fishing at the widest point. At least, there used to be. I haven't been in years."

"But my other grandpa used to take her there." Jayda tugged Rance's folks toward the river. "When we lived in Dallas and he came to visit, we fished in a reservoir."

"Well, lead the way." Rance's mother waved to him and Larae as Jayda barreled toward the woods.

"Slow down, Jayda." Larae shielded her eyes from the sun. "Don't drag them."

Jayda slowed to a fast walk.

"I think they can handle her. They walk two miles a day since Dad's cholesterol wake-up call."

"I didn't know about that." Larae's concern softened her features. "Are you sure he'll be all right?"

"He's in the best shape he's been in years thanks to Mom's strict exercise regime and lean meals."

"Let me talk to the guys, go over final details, and then I'll be there."

"Listen, if you want to stay and supervise here, I can distract Jayda."

"Don't try to cut me out of the outing." Her gaze narrowed.

"That's not what I'm doing. Talking about the river seemed to bring back memories for you. I just thought you might not be comfortable with it."

"I'm fine. They were good memories." Her eyes turned cold. "Mostly good anyway."

And her meaning was obvious. She wished she'd never snuck down to the river to meet him.

"If you're sure, I'll get the gear."

"It'll take lots of gear." She dug in her pocket, pulled out a bundle of keys, slipped off one and held it toward him. "Load it into the mule. It's in the shed, too. Should be gassed up and ready to go."

"I'll wait for you."

"There's no need."

"Larae. I'm not going without you."

Her gaze measured him. "If you insist."

"I do."

She turned away and hurried to speak with the work crew's foreman.

One thing was sure. If they were going to do this parenting thing together, they had to count on each other. But how could he get her to trust him? Without revealing what had happened with her dad. The man she still had on a pedestal.

Larae was halfway to the shed when the low rumble of the mule started up.

Seconds later, Rance pulled out and drove up to her. "Your chariot awaits."

Oh, how she'd rather walk. But she couldn't let him know the thought of sitting beside him bothered her. She crawled in next to him.

He sat there, idling. "I want what's best for Jayda."

"I do, too."

"I need you to trust me with her." His gaze snagged hers. "Trust that I won't do anything to hurt her, try to exclude you when I spend time with her, or try to monopolize her. That I won't intentionally do anything to hurt you. Or your reputation."

"That all sounds good."

"And I need you to do the same. We need to raise her together and put her best interest first."

"I agree." Her heart did a painful flip-flop. She'd have to share Jayda from now on.

"I need you to stop always thinking the worst of me, assuming I'm up to something or have ulterior motives."

"I'll try."

"I know I hurt you once. But I was a kid. I'm not anymore. How can I prove to you that I've changed?"

"Just don't let Jayda down. All I want is for her to be happy and loved."

"Me, too." He offered his hand. "Shake on it."

She wanted to trust his offer, but touching him always did funny things to her insides. Hesitantly, she clasped his hand. And every nerve ending went on high alert.

"All right, let's not keep our Baby Girl waiting." He drove toward the river, avoiding clumps of prickly pear cactus as they went.

She liked the way he said *our* instead of *my*. Could she really trust this guy? Had he changed? With all her Rance-entangled heart, she hoped so.

"Mommy! Daddy!" Jayda jumped up and down, jerking her fishing line with each bounce. "You came."

"We said we would." Rance gathered the extra rods and reels along with a tackle box.

"I know, but I figured it would take *forever*." Jayda drew the word out with dramatic flourish. "When Mommy says in a few minutes, that means at least thirty minutes to an hour."

Larae's face heated.

"Well, your mama's a very busy lady." Rance ambled down the path to where white river rocks lined the water. "And she's always had to do everything on her own and take care of you all by herself. Maybe since I'm here now, I can help her get stuff done so we can both spend more time with you."

Rance defending her? Her heart warmed.

"Yay." Jayda clapped her hands and dropped her pole. As she did, it slowly dragged toward the water.

"You got a bite, Baby Girl." Rance dove for the pole and snagged it just before it disappeared into the water. "Help me reel her in."

He made a big show of struggling with the fish as if Jaws was on the other end of the line, but when it popped out of the water, it was small.

"Look at that bass, Baby Girl. You caught that all by yourself."

"It's tiny, Daddy. I can do a whole lot better than that."

"Well, can you now?"

"Whoever catches the biggest fish gets to eat it." Jayda grinned.

"You're on, Baby Girl."

Larae watched as her little girl blossomed under the attention of Rance and his parents. Had she failed Jayda in keeping her away from this family all these years? When Jayda got old enough to understand everything, would she resent Larae for keeping her a secret?

All she could do was allow Jayda to spend plenty of time with Rance and her new grandparents to make up for the time they'd lost.

And pray Rance would stay put like he'd promised and not break Jayda's heart by leaving. Since she was attending church again, like God wanted, she prayed a lot these days. Now she just needed Him to answer.

The arena enclosure was updated, reinforced and fully in place the next afternoon when Rance strolled down Larae's drive. He'd gotten tied up on the phone most of the day. In the process, he'd missed Jayda before she went to school and hadn't been here when she'd gotten home. And he hadn't liked it at all. She made him want to forget about his business and spend every spare minute with her.

Larae and Jayda exited the house and headed for the SUV.

"Hey." He waved. "Where are y'all going?"

"We're putting out more flyers." Jayda held up a handful as he jogged to catch up with them. "Want to come with us?"

Now who was trying to exclude who? "More flyers?"

"These advertise the starting date." Larae handed him one.

Their fingers touched, sending fireworks through his nerve endings.

"That it's a done deal, gonna happen. I almost called

you, but since we hadn't seen you all day, I figured you were busy."

And she'd probably been glad, hoping to slip away without him.

"I was on the phone with a breeder most of the day." He scanned the flyer. "In two weeks? Isn't that rushing things a bit?"

"I figure the sooner we get started the better. I have all the staff in place. The arena, all the chutes, the concession stand, the bathrooms, announcer's booth and seating will be finished by then. Everything is on schedule."

"What if there's a flood and it's not finished in time? We've got a lot of ranchers around here praying for rain."

"Then we'll advertise a new date. The ranch needs this."

"I know. But you can't control the weather, Larae."

"No. But I know who can. As dry as it is, I'm not praying against rain. But I am praying He'll work it out."

Larae praying?

"She's been doing that since we went to church with you, Daddy. And I really like it when Mommy prays."

"Me, too," he admitted as he sought Larae's gaze. Had one Sunday changed her mind about church? If anyone could, his caring church family could.

"We're going to Bible study with you tomorrow night, too," Jayda said.

"If that's okay with you." Larae ducked her head, almost shy.

"Of course. Anytime."

"Mommy said we're gonna start going all the time."

"Well, I'm tickled about that."

"Can you come with us to put the new fliers up, Daddy?"

"I wouldn't miss it." An evening spent with his two favorite girls.

But he couldn't think that way about Larae. She was

just as off-limits as she'd been in high school. Focus on Jayda. Not her far too appealing mother.

Over the next few hours, they left flyers in the few businesses in Medina and covered the stores in Comfort. With Jayda's hand in his and Larae strolling along beside him, it was one of the best days he could remember.

"Ooh, that's pretty." Jayda pointed at a turquoise bracelet as they turned to leave one of the gift shops. Each tiny stone formed the middle of a silver flower.

"I think you need it. What do you think?" He shot her a wink.

"Oh yes, Daddy, please."

"It's kind of expensive, Jayda." Larae shook her head at him. "It would be terrible if you lost it."

"I won't. I still have the ring Grandpa Collins got me for Christmas before last." She held her hand up to reveal an opal.

"It's not a big deal." Rance slid the bracelet off the display. "I'd really like to get it for her. But it's your call."

Her gaze narrowed, fully aware that if she didn't let him, she'd be the bad guy in Jayda's eyes. He needed to work on that. On thinking first with Jayda instead of always opening up his big mouth and making Larae mad at every turn.

"I suppose it's okay. Just this once. But you can't buy everything she wants."

"Mommy says I'll get spoiled and grow up to be good-for-nothing if I never have to work for anything."

Rance grinned. "She's right."

"You can have the bracelet, Jayda. And since it's real turquoise, let's just wear it to church and for special occasions when you won't be running and playing. That way it won't get lost. You'll have to be careful like you are with your ring."

Her commitment to church attendance warmed his heart.

"Okay, Mommy. Can I wear it today?"

"If you'll be careful."

He slipped the bracelet on Jayda's wrist and clasped it in place, then opened his wallet and handed the cashier the bills.

"Look, it fits perfect." Jayda shook her arm. "It's not big enough to slide over my hand."

"It looks very pretty." Larae looked up at him. "Thank you. What do you say, Jayda?"

"Thank you, Daddy." She plowed into his middle with a hug. "I love it."

"Looks like it was made for you, Baby Girl."

Larae checked her watch. "We need to go home. It's almost time for supper, and Stella insisted on cooking for us."

"You're right." He opened the door, and Jayda skipped out ahead of them, still admiring her bracelet.

"Watch where you're going, Jayda," Larae called. "And don't get too far away from us."

"Okay, Mommy."

"I'm sorry about the bracelet," Rance whispered.

"I've worked really hard at not spoiling her."

"And you've done a great job. I didn't mean to make you the bad guy. I promise I'll work on thinking first with her in the future."

"I'd appreciate that."

Her tone was abrupt. Would he ever get anywhere with Larae? Get her to trust him? At the rate he was going, not for a very long time.

Chapter Twelve

In two days, they'd replaced all the initial rodeo flyers with the grand opening ones and alerted the radio stations. Except for the ones they'd put in San Antonio. Larae couldn't face that drive alone with Rance, so she'd sneak off by herself when she could.

They'd gotten back in time to pick Jayda up from school and take her with them to hang flyers in Bandera.

"So we're all done. Anybody hungry?"

"Me. Me. Me." Jayda stuck her hand up in the back seat.

"Remember, we have church tonight." Larae's stomach rumbled right on cue.

"Sounds like your mama is, too." He checked his watch. "We've got time. How about the O.S.T."

"What's that?" Jayda asked.

"It stands for Old Spanish Trail." Larae looked out the window. If not for her traitorous gut, they could have gone home to eat. And gotten rid of Rance quicker. "It's a restaurant with yummy food."

"I can't believe you've never taken her there."

"We lived in Dallas. Dad came to visit us there. I never brought Jayda here." To keep him in the dark about her. A decision she was beginning to regret.

"Well, it's high time she went." His tone was solid—no trace of anger. He was obviously trying hard to put their past behind them. He found a parking slot at the other end of the block and pulled in. "O.S.T. is right down the street."

Spending time with him wasn't terrible, apart from watching Jayda flourish in his attention and hearing her sing his praises. If he ever let her little girl down, Larae would find a way to make his life miserable.

They strolled the strip of sidewalk, then stepped inside, and Jayda looked around, making Larae remember the first time she'd seen it. Younger than Jayda, she'd come here with her parents, and it had become their go-to place to eat out. The huge wagon wheel light fixture, the salad bar housed in a covered wagon, sets of longhorns on the walls.

"I wanna sit on the saddle stools."

"Sounds like a plan." Rance ushered Larae to follow their child.

"What kind of deer is that?" Jayda's eyes widened at the huge antlers behind the serving bar.

"It's an elk."

A waitress ducked under the elk to give them menus.

"It's the hugest thing I've ever seen." Jayda clapped her hands.

"I think *hugest* is the perfect word for it." Rance shot her a wink.

They placed their orders, and it wasn't long before their food came.

"Wow, I forgot how big the fish and shrimp are here." Larae homed in on his plate.

"That catfish takes up half your plate, Daddy. And I think they might have given you chicken legs instead of shrimp."

The waitress laughed. "You let me know if you need any more chicken legs."

Rance reached for Larae's hand across the bar in front of Jayda sitting between them.

Her first instinct was to jerk away. Instead, she caught his gaze.

"Let's pray. I usually pray before I eat."

"Oh." She clasped his hand. Shock waves went straight to her heart. Jayda's small hand slipped into her free one. But Larae didn't hear any of the prayer. And when Rance let go, her hand went cold.

Jayda and Rance dug into their plates, but, even though she was hungry and the food was excellent, Larae merely nibbled at her burger and onion rings.

"Are you the one starting a rodeo in Medina?" a male voice asked from her left.

"Yes." She turned to see a man in his midthirties, decked out in cowboy gear.

"You're Clay Warren." Rance's jaw dropped. "My dad and I followed your career from beginning to end. You were the greatest."

"Now I don't know about that." Mr. Warren ducked his head. "But I gave it a good run."

"This is Clay Warren." Shock echoed in Rance's words. "He won the CBR World title four times."

"What's that?" Jayda stuck a fry in her mouth.

"Championship Bull Riding," Larae explained.

Jayda's eyes widened. "You ride bulls."

"I used to. But not anymore."

"How come?"

"Jayda, remember it's not polite to ask personal questions."

"It's okay." Clay grinned. "I got married and had a little girl and bull riding's kind of dangerous, so I traded in my boots for my family."

"We're starting a rodeo."

"I know. Do you have a start date yet?"

"The twenty-ninth of this month." Larae handed him one of her new business cards with her number and address. "That's where we're building. It will be outdoor until we can get the indoor site up and running."

"That's great news." Clay tucked the card in his shirt pocket. "I've always thought Medina needed a rodeo."

"Do you live near?"

"No. But my grandfather does."

"My dad has breakfast here with a group of men, including your grandpa." Rance looked like he might have to pinch himself to make sure this was real.

"He really enjoys those gatherings."

"Do you think y'all could come to our rodeo?" Jayda asked. "It's gonna be really good. Mommy's good at heading up rodeos."

"Well, I don't know about that." Larae blushed. "I'm good at publicizing them once they're already up and running. How did you find out about my rodeo?"

"I saw the flyer in the window and asked the waitress who was behind it. She pointed you out. I won't be in town for your grand opening, but I'll try to make one next time I'm here." He offered his hand. "It was nice meeting y'all."

"Nice meeting you. And I hope you can make it." Larae clasped his hand. "Please tell all your friends."

"I'll be sure to." He shook hands with Rance and went back to his table.

"I'll never wash my hand again," Rance muttered.

"You're silly, Daddy." Jayda giggled.

"Do you have any idea what this means?" Larae stared off into space.

"I just met Clay Warren."

"If he comes to our rodeo, he could put us on the map."

"They're putting our rodeo on the map?" Jayda wiped her mouth with her napkin.

"It's a figure of speech, sweetie. It means Clay Warren fans would hear about our rodeo."

"And he has a lot of fans."

"Are they all goofy about it, like you, Daddy?"

"Not as goofy as I am over you, Baby Girl." He leaned in and kissed the top of Jayda's head.

Larae's heart did a somersault. Loving her daughter was the quickest way to her heart. But she couldn't fall for Rance. Not again.

Next door was like a magnet for Rance. He strolled down the long drive and caught sight of Larae and Jayda at the barn. Several workers installed sections of the new bucking chutes and pens, with the hum of heavy equipment covering his approach. It was early enough that the heat hadn't set in yet.

He couldn't stay away. What had he done all these years without Jayda? Without Larae?

Having them at Bible study with him last night was like a balm to his soul. Jayda had gone to the kids' class with Amelia while Larae had seemed completely comfortable and settled in. Everyone treated them like a family. If only that was the truth.

If he kept showing up unannounced, Larae was liable to give him his walking papers or set up some annoying schedule for him to visit Jayda. But he was helping with the rodeo, which would speed things along and benefit him, too.

Maybe someday soon she'd let Jayda come to his house, but he wouldn't hold his breath.

As he neared, he could see Larae and Jayda were in a pen with a rust-colored calf.

A twig snapped under his foot, and they both looked up. Jayda's eyes danced. Larae's steamed.

"Look, Daddy, I'm feeding Little Bit." Jayda held an oversize bottle while the calf tugged and sucked on the nipple, almost toppling her.

"Careful there, big boy." Rance slipped through the gate and put his hands on his daughter's shoulders to steady her.

"His mama had twins, but she's not feeding this one. It's like he doesn't have a mommy. Isn't that sad?"

"It is sad." He caught Larae's gaze and got a glimpse of the wounded, motherless little girl inside her.

"But I'm helping Denny take care of him."

"You sure are."

The calf sucked the bottle dry and kept tugging.

"I think he wants more."

"If we give him too much at a time, he might get a tummy ache," Larae cautioned. "We'll feed him again at lunch."

"But I'll be at school at lunchtime."

"You can feed him again at supper." Rance helped her tug the bottle free of the calf, then turned to Larae. "What's on the agenda today?"

"Tons of phone calls." She rolled her eyes. "I'm hitting up businesses for sponsorships."

"I can split the list with you." They exited the pen and Rance secured the gate.

"I don't know. Have you ever done anything like this?"

"Not necessarily, but I can be very persuasive. And with me helping, you can finish quicker and squeeze in some Jayda time after school."

"Grandma and Grandpa are here." Jayda jumped up and down.

Larae smiled, sending his heart into overdrive.

His dad parked, and his parents climbed out of the car.

"I thought we might take Jayda to school," his mom said as she waved. "I hope that's okay."

"Of course it is."

Jayda ran to greet them, and his dad picked her up.

"Mommy and Daddy are making calls today, and Mr. Denny is busy with the horses. I'm supposed to stay with Miss Stella after school, but can I stay with y'all instead?"

"Jayda, we've talked about inviting yourself over."

"I'm sorry, Mommy." She turned hopeful eyes on his mother. "But can I?"

"Jayda!" Larae chastened.

"Your mommy's right about inviting yourself to someone's house." His father pressed his nose to hers. "But it doesn't count with us. If it's okay with your mommy, you can come over anytime."

"It's fine by me." Larae leaned against the calf-pen railing.

"But what about feeding Little Bit at supper?"

"You'll be home in plenty of time."

"We could take Jayda to school and pick her up each day," His father offered. "At least while you're swamped with rodeo business."

"Oh, I couldn't let you do that. It's too much."

"We don't mind at all." His mother did a one-shoulder shrug. "It gives us something to do. And we love spending time with this one."

"Maybe. At least part of the time."

"Okay. Let's go." Jayda gripped each grandparent by the hand and tugged them toward their car.

"Slow down, Jayda. Don't jerk Mr. and Mrs. Shepherd around."

"I think we're past *Mr.* and *Mrs.*" His mom patted Larae's shoulder. "Please call us Maggie and Davis. And if you're sure you don't mind us whisking this little darling away, we'll do just that."

"Do you want to take some toys or coloring books, Jayda? Grandma and Grandpa probably don't have any at their house."

"Except, we do." His dad grimaced. "We kind of went shopping so Jayda wouldn't be bored at our place. I hope you don't mind."

"It's fine." Larae shrugged. "It'll make things easier if we don't have to drag her stuff back and forth."

"But Mommy doesn't want you to spoil me so I'll be worth something someday."

His father chuckled. "Sounds like you have a very smart mommy. You better give her a hug before we go."

She hugged Larae. And then Rance. His heart puddled at her feet.

After a round of goodbyes, his parents drove off with Jayda waving from the back window of their car.

"How come you're fine with my folks spending time with Jayda, but not so much with me?"

"Because Jayda needs family. My dad was all I had, and he's gone. And your parents have lived in the same place for as long as I can remember. I don't see them pulling up stakes and leaving her behind."

"I'm not planning to, either. I told you that."

"You told me a lot of things back in high school." Her gaze hardened, and she headed to the house. "We'll see if you mean what you say this time."

But he had meant everything he'd told her back then. How could he convince her to trust him without knocking her dad off the pedestal she'd put him on?

He followed her to the house. Inside, it was warm and cozy. The walls were lined with family pictures of Larae and her parents, then just her and her dad. But nothing as an adult and none of Jayda.

"Why aren't there any pictures of Jayda?"

"Because the only people from Medina who knew she existed were Dad and Lexie. I sent Dad photo albums, but he kept them hidden."

"Where? I'd love to see her baby pictures. I've missed so much."

Her eyes softened. "I'm not sure." She opened a door at the bottom of a bookcase and pulled out several photo albums, flipped through them and set each aside. "Jayda was the sweetest baby. She hardly ever cried."

"Were you alone? I mean when you had her?"

She looked up at him. "No. Lexie stayed with me. I couldn't have gone through it without her."

"I'm glad. I hate to think of you being alone."

"Here's one. And this one. And here's another." She put the non-Jayda ones back. "I think that's all. You can take them home with you if you want. And once you look through them, bring them back, and I'll make copies for you."

"Will it put you behind schedule if I look at them now?" He sat down on the couch, unable to accomplish anything else until he saw the pictures.

"No. Go right ahead. I'll have to go back to Dallas before the start of June and get the rest of our things from our condo. I have lots more there." She set the other albums beside him and turned toward the office, then stopped, came back and settled on the couch beside him. "They're in order from pre-birth to last fall."

He opened the album as if it were a sacred relic. Grainy ultrasound pictures.

"This is six weeks. It's hard to tell anything, but she's right here." She pointed to a tiny bean-shaped object.

He flipped the page. Pictures of Larae, obviously pregnant. The Larae he fell in love with. Carrying his child. If only he'd known, everything would be so different now. "Were you scared?"

"Terrified. I knew nothing about babies. I was in a city where I knew no one, and I was trying to keep up in my college courses."

"Where did you live?" It didn't look like a dorm.

"With a friend Dad grew up with. He and his wife rented rooms out of their home once their kids were grown and gone. Lola and Al became like grandparents to me."

"Did your dad visit often?" In each pregnancy picture, she was smiling, but her eyes were haunted by fear.

"He ended up coming and staying for the last three

months of my pregnancy. And once Jayda was born, Lola taught us how to take care of her. Dad and I were both clueless."

"Was there a lot of pain?"

"Oh, my. You can't imagine. But once I saw her, it faded to a memory."

The next page was filled by a tiny baby with a puff of dark hair—a baby that turned his insides to jelly.

"So worth it." Larae touched a fingertip to the image of Jayda's baby face. "Her hair was like that when she was born. Three inches long all over her head. It stayed that dark until she was about two, then it just kept getting lighter and lighter."

The next several pages were of Jayda napping, smiling. Pictures of Larae holding her with the haunting fear in her eyes replaced by joy. Pictures of Ray holding her, completely captivated.

The same way Jayda made Rance feel.

"This is Lola and Al." She pointed to a picture of a smiling older couple holding Jayda. "Lola is the one who led me to Christ after Jayda was born. I wish I'd gotten back into church then." She sighed. "Once I finished my degree and got my own place, they came to visit often."

"I'm glad you weren't alone."

They finished the first album. In the second, Jayda turned into a happy blond toddler.

"That's Punk, her favorite stuffed animal." Larae pointed to the pink dog. "I'm not sure if she was trying to say *pink* or *pumpkin*, since I've always called her Pumpkin. Dad got him for her, and she's slept with him since."

As he turned the pages, Larae told him the story of each picture—Jayda's age, where they were, what they were doing. It filled in some gaps for him. But he wasn't sure if he felt better or worse since he hadn't been there.

"This was the first time I took her to ride at the stables in Dallas. She was three."

And looked like a two-year-old. So tiny. "Wasn't she too small to be riding?"

"I started when I was three and was about the same size. She had a helmet, see. And a very good instructor." She flipped the page for him. "This is her first trip to the zoo."

Jayda was in a stroller and Ray was pushing her. With all their outings, it seemed like they'd have run into someone from Medina. But even if they had, no one would have figured out that Jayda was his.

They finished the second album. The third held pictures showing first days of school, Jayda with friends and at birthday parties, and Jayda at the rodeo with Larae.

Since Rance's boss at the time had stocked the rodeo Larae had worked for, it's a wonder they hadn't run into each other there. If only they had.

Easter pictures, Christmas photos, picnics in the park. All with one common theme. No Rance.

"I wish I'd been there."

She sighed, closing the final album. "I'm sorry, Rance. I really didn't think you'd want to be in her life. I didn't mean to hurt you."

"I didn't mean to hurt you, either."

"What do you say we do our best to stop hurting each other?"

"I'm in."

"Good." She bumped his shoulder with hers. "I have some DVDs of her, too. They're still in Dallas, but when I get my stuff, you can watch them if you want."

"Please. Mom and Dad will want to see them, too. Along with the albums."

"Once I get my albums from the condo, you can actually have these. With Dad gone, they're just collecting dust."

"Thanks." But pictures and DVDs didn't change the

fact that he hadn't been there for the first seven years of Jayda's life.

In fact, the pictures only highlighted his absence. And the DVDs would, too. Rance could never get those years back. Or make up for them.

All he could do was make the most of the time he had with her now. And in the future.

Chapter Thirteen

Day two of calling sponsors, and Rance had already landed several. Seated across the conference table from Larae, he continued to surprise her.

Outside, the concession stand and bathrooms were under construction, and the plumber was scheduled for tomorrow. Everything was right on schedule. So far.

Rance ended his call. "Good news."

"What's that?"

"With all these sponsorships piling up, I figure we need a graphics guy, right?"

"Right."

"I know a guy. Chris Tilton. Remember him from school?"

"I do. He did all the signage for the rodeo I was with when we lived in Dallas."

"So I called him. He offered to make all the signs and banners we'll need, now and in the future, in exchange for a free sign advertising his business to grace our arenas indefinitely. What do you think?"

"I know he's reliable." It was all she could do to focus and keep her mind on the rodeo and not Rance. "Sounds like a great deal to me. We'd spend way more than the cost of a sponsorship in the long run."

"Great. I'll call him back to accept."

But before he could dial, the house phone he was manning rang.

"Collins Ranch. May I help you?" He paused. "That's right, if you sponsor the outdoor arena, your sponsorship transfers to the indoor rodeo once it's up and running, but your sign will still hang in the outdoor arena, which will be a rentable practice space. So you'll get a two for one in the long run." Rance shot her a thumbs-up and quoted their price. "And that's for the whole year.

"Great. I'll send you an email with an invoice. Once you send me your graphics, I'll get it to our designer. We'll send you a proof for approval, and your sign will hang in the arena for our grand opening in one week. Yes. Thank you." He ended the call. "Word's getting around. That was the feed store in Bandera. The hardware store owner told him about us, so all I had to do was close the deal. I think I'm getting the hang of this."

"Well, you learned from one of the best."

"And humblest, too."

"Just confident."

"How many more do we need?"

"That's all for the outdoor arena." She checked her chart for the layout of the indoor building. "We have room for ten more indoors."

"So I guess we wait until the building's finished for that?"

"No, we keep doing what we're doing and get it all booked."

"How? We have nothing to offer them now."

"We convince them they need it. And we're talking a matter of months." She dialed a number, then leaned back in her chair and put her bare feet, crossed at the ankles, up on the conference table. "Watch this."

"Yes. Mr. Townsend, this is Larae Collins. I hope I'm not catching you at a bad time."

"Not at all. It's good to hear from you, Miss Collins."

"I thought you'd want to know about a new rodeo starting up on property I own in Medina. We're calling it the Collins Family Rodeo, and no alcoholic beverages will be served. Now, I'm having my grand opening at our outdoor arena the end of this month, but I'm sorry to report that I'm out of sponsorship opportunities for that."

She was back in her element, despite her erratic heartbeat. Maybe it was excitement about the rodeo and nothing to do with Rance.

"I'd have liked to get in on that."

"Well, here's your chance." She slid her feet off the table and leaned forward in her chair to look at her chart. "I'm building an indoor arena, as well. It will be finished by early summer. Just in time to beat the heat, right?" She chuckled. "I'm running out of slots, but I knew you'd want to get in on this. My prime slot is below the announcers booth."

"A prime slot, indeed." Interest echoed in his voice.

She had him right where she wanted him. "Now, I also have other slots that cost less, but I know *Go Big Or Go Home* is your motto, so I saved my prime opportunity for you." The price she named was exorbitant, higher than the other slots.

"For a prime slot, that sounds reasonable. Count me in."

"Perfect." She wrote *Townsend Gas & Oil* on her chart. "I'll send you an email with the invoice. We've got time, but as soon as you send me your graphics, I'll get my designer on it. Thank you very much, Mr. Townsend." She shot Rance a satisfied grin. "It's my honor to be part of your advertising team. We'll speak soon." She ended the call. "And that's how it's done."

"My hat's off to you. Literally." He took his Stetson off, set it on the table and raked his fingers through his hair. "You didn't even ask him if he wanted it."

"Marketing 101. Convince them they have to have it."

"Mommy, Daddy, are you finished yet?" Jayda scampered into the office.

And Larae's heart went soft.

"Time to call it a day." Larae checked her watch and turned her chair around. Rance's folks had agreed to take Jayda to school and pick her up, then spend a little time with her before bringing her home. It was tempting to take them up on their offer of doing the same every day since she and Rance had gotten so much accomplished today. Except she'd missed Jayda.

"Let's go on a picnic." Jayda plopped in her lap.

"That sounds perfect." At least, it would be if they were really a family.

"I'm in." Rance retrieved his Stetson.

"I'll see what I can find to pack our basket." Larae gave Jayda a hug.

"Miss Stella already did it. It was her idea. She says you and Daddy work too much and we need some family time."

So now Stella was conspiring against her. "I'm not sure about that. But let me go change into some shorts, and we'll go."

"Hurry, Mommy."

"I will."

What she wouldn't give to have a real family for her little girl.

Rance unpacked the veritable feast from the picnic basket packed to the brim. "I'm liking Miss Stella more and more all the time."

"Have you ever met Miss Stella, Daddy?"

"A long time ago. I worked for your grandpa for a while here at the ranch. That's how I met your mama." But all he could really think about was how cute Larae looked in her pink top and white shorts, with shimmery toes that matched her shirt. Tiny and determined. A force to be reckoned with. Especially where his heart was concerned.

"I didn't know that, Daddy. Miss Stella is awesome. She cooks for everybody and watches me when Mommy's working and helps Mommy keep the house clean."

"I think I might need a Miss Stella at my place."

"She is awesome." Larae gazed off in the distance. "After my mom died, Stella became my stand-in mom. I can't believe I stayed away from this place—from these people—for so long."

"Why did you, Mommy?"

Larae's cheeks went crimson.

"Your mommy had a really good job in Dallas, and she had you to take care of." He was getting good at covering for Larae, for Jayda's peace of mind.

But no matter how cute Larae was or the number she did on his heart, she still thought he was a jerk and he still didn't have enough money to even think about pursuing her.

"Maybe if we'd come back here sooner, I would have met you quicker, Daddy."

Longing for those lost years made his eyes burn. "Probably not. I traveled the rodeo circuit most of the years y'all lived in Dallas and only moved back here a few months ago." If only he and Larae had bumped into each other at the rodeo during those years.

"So you moved home and then Mommy did. It's like God arranged it so we could know about each other."

His heart squeezed. "You're probably right, Baby Girl."

A snort sounded from behind them. In unison, they turned, searching for the source of the noise.

A massive black bull with his head lowered. Rance's blood went cold.

"Is he about to—" Larae's voice quivered.

"Yes. The fence on our right is closest. I'll carry Jayda."

"I can get her."

"This is no time to argue," he hissed. "I've got her. Run." He snatched Jayda up as the bull pawed the ground.

Larae ran ahead. Thundering hooves sounded behind them. Jayda screamed.

"It's okay. I've got you." He caught up with Larae, even carrying his extra load. He could easily outrun her, make certain Jayda was safe. But what about the woman he'd loved since high school? He caught her hand and dragged her along. "Hurry, Larae."

They made it to the rail fence and clambered over. The bull was only yards away, still coming fast and hard.

He spotted a large live oak with lots of massive low limbs. "Get behind that tree in case he comes through. We'll climb it if we have to."

They scurried behind the tree and watched with bated breath. The bull turned just before slamming into the fence, roared back the way he'd come, then slowed and came to a stop. He pawed, shook his head and started grazing.

"It's okay, Baby Girl." He patted Jayda's back. With her face pressed into his neck, she shuddered. "Daddy's got you, we're safe."

"Give her to me." Larae grabbed for her.

But Jayda stayed balled up against him. "Let's get her home, then I'll tend to the bull."

"That's your bull?"

"Yes."

"What are you thinking keeping a bull like that?"

"He's a rodeo bull, Larae. They're mean. It's part of the sport."

"But Jayda lives here."

"Yes, she does. And I kept her safe. I'll see to it that none of my stock gets out again. If I have to build a concrete wall, I will."

"I watched it the whole time." Jayda sniffled. "From

over your shoulder, Daddy. It wanted to get us. To get all of us."

"I know, Pumpkin." Larae hugged Jayda's back. "It's okay. We're all safe. Daddy kept us safe."

"Mommy, I was so scared."

"I know, but we're okay."

Jayda pushed away from him, reaching for Larae.

"Take her home. I'll take care of the bull."

"No, Daddy. It'll get you."

"It won't, Baby Girl. I'm not going back in the field with it. I'll go over to my place and put feed in its pen. It'll come, and I'll stay safe. I promise."

"Okay." Jayda buried her face in Larae's hair.

Why did he feel like the worst dad in the world?

Chapter Fourteen

Jayda's breaths evened out in rhythmic slumber against Larae's shoulder. The doorbell rang just as she'd gotten comfortable in the twin bed. Probably Rance. What had taken him so long? Didn't he ever stop to think how late it was, that Jayda was probably asleep? If she ignored him, he'd just keep ringing and wake Jayda.

She kept an eye on Jayda, sat up without jiggling the bed, then eased off the mattress. Slipping into her robe, she tiptoed out of the room and scurried down the stairs.

The bell rang again just before she got to it. She undid the lock and flung the door open.

"Jayda's asleep," she snapped. "If you didn't wake her up, that is."

"Sorry, I just wanted to see about her."

"It took her forever to go to sleep, and the only reason she did was because I promised to stay in her room all night. And now I've broken my promise because of you. So go home and let me go back to her. Besides, if you were really that worried, what took you so long?"

"For your information, the bull didn't want to go back into his pen. Not even for food. I repaired the board that let him out, then reinforced the rest of the pens so it won't happen again. I finally got him back in just a few minutes ago."

"You can go now."

"Mommy!" Jayda's wail coursed adrenaline through Larae.

She bolted for the stairs. "It's okay, sweetie. I'm coming."

"Mommy!" Jayda was curled in a ball, holding Punk the pink dog.

"It's okay, sweetie. I'm right here." Larae gathered her up in her arms.

"I had a dream." She hiccuped a sob. "About the bull. And you weren't here." She pulled away to look up at Larae with tears rolling down her cheeks.

"I'm sorry, Baby Girl. Your mama only left to let me in."

"Daddy." Jayda reached for him.

He settled on the bed and pulled the trembling little body into his chest. Completely out of place in the pink-and-purple room decorated with princesses and crowns.

"I dreamed the bull got you after we left."

"I'm fine. I got it back in its pen and reinforced all the wood, so it won't get out again. In fact, I'm calling a guy tomorrow about steel pens instead of wood so none of my bulls will ever get out again."

"Is there gonna be bulls at our rodeo, Mommy?"

"Yes." Larae winced. "But that's why the arena guys were here. They made sure the railing was strong enough to hold them. And we'll have steel pens, so there won't be anything to worry about."

"I don't know if I want a rodeo anymore."

"I thought you loved rodeos, Pumpkin. You always wanted to come to work with me."

"They always kind of scared me. I just liked being with you."

Larae's eyes felt scalded. How could she not have realized that? "Well, when we get our rodeo, if you want to skip the bulls, you can."

"I never wanna see another one. Ever."

"You don't have to." Rance patted her back. "Why don't you try to go back to sleep? It's late."

"I can't." Her arms tightened around his neck.

"Yes, you can. It was just a nightmare. We're all safe. And now that you know I'm all right, you'll be able to sleep."

"Will you stay here in my room, too, Daddy?"

Larae's eyes went wide, begging him not to agree.

"There's nowhere for me to sleep."

"You can sleep in the recliner. Mommy says it's really comfy."

"Daddy has to go, Pumpkin."

"I can't sleep if we're not all here. I'll have another dream about the bull." She pulled away and looked up at him with tear-filled eyes. "I just know it."

Larae watched him cave.

"You know, I saw a comfy-looking couch downstairs."

Larae shook her head at him, giving him her best evil eye.

"I want you closer, Daddy. You can sleep in the guest room right across the hall. With the door open."

"I'll do whatever it takes to keep my Baby Girl happy."

Whether Larae liked it or not. She'd been in complete control where Jayda was concerned up until recently. He obviously thought it was his turn now.

Unable to sleep with Rance lurking so near, Larae had stayed awake half the night, long after soft snores echoed from across the hall. Afraid to move and wake Jayda, she'd never gotten comfortable.

When she awoke, her hip was cramped from staying in the same position all night. Jayda was still asleep beside her. At least the poor baby hadn't had any more nightmares about bulls or anything else. Larae listened for Rance's snoring and didn't hear it. Was he already downstairs? Or gone?

Sunlight streamed through the curtains. She longed to look at her watch to see what time it was. At least it was Saturday and Jayda didn't have school.

It was tempting to clear her calendar, but she needed to set up and organize the concession stand today. Jayda could help her. Maybe being inside the structure would make her feel secure.

Jayda's eyes popped open. "Mommy."

"Hey, sweetie."

"Thanks for staying with me all night." She snuggled close.

"Anytime." It hadn't been the first time and probably wouldn't be the last. But they'd never had a third wheel before.

Jayda's eyes widened. "Is Daddy still here?"

"I sure am, Baby Girl." Rance's voice came from the guest room.

The warm bundle pulled away, sat up and headed to the door. Larae wanted to shout at him to get out.

Rance scooped Jayda up and swung her around. Larae sat up, then stood and tried to smooth the wrinkles out of her modest pink top and capris pajamas with crowns, high heels and princesses dotting the fabric.

"How about I fix breakfast for you?"

"Pancakes?" Jayda perked up a little.

"Definitely."

And she was stuck with him.

"Why don't you change?" He scanned Larae's pajamas, and his grin widened. "I'll take Jayda down with me."

"What? Have you never seen adult princess pajamas?"

"I have a matching pair." Jayda pulled out of his arms and twirled for him to see. "Maybe we can get you some prince pajamas, Daddy."

"I'd wear them for you, Baby Girl." He chuckled.

"I know, Daddy."

He headed downstairs with Larae's heart in his arms. She blew out a big breath and dug through her closet.

Twenty minutes later, dressed and wearing light makeup, she entered the kitchen.

Jayda was already eating her pancakes with Stella sitting across from her.

What would Stella think? Larae's face heated. With Rance's wrinkled clothes, it was obvious he'd been here all night.

"Morning, Stella."

"Morning. I can't remember the last time anyone cooked me breakfast. I'm liking this man of yours."

"He's not my man." Her cheeks scalded. "He slept in the guest room. Only because Jayda had a nightmare."

"Relax. Rance already explained. But I assumed you two were working on getting back together?"

"I wish." Jayda's voice turned wistful.

"Well, we're not. Daddy is only here for you, Jayda."

"Right." Rance shot Jayda a wink.

"Are you finished eating, Pumpkin?"

"Uh-huh."

"Why don't you get dressed?"

Jayda slipped out of her chair. "Are we still working on the concession stand today?"

"We are. Maybe we can take care of the concession stuff quickly and go fishing or do something else fun." Larae gave her a hug.

"I'll run home and take a shower, then be back to help." Rance ushered Jayda toward the stairs. "Larae, there's a pan staying warm for you in the oven."

Stella hopped up and used a hot pad to get the dish, then set it on the table in front of Larae.

Eggs, bacon and pancakes. Still warm. "I could have gotten it. Finish your breakfast."

"He's a good guy, you know." Stella forked a bite of pancake.

"He has his moments."

"You could have told me you were pregnant when you left. I wish you had."

"I was embarrassed. And I didn't want Rance to know."

"Why?"

"He——" She chose her words carefully. "He'd proven I couldn't depend on him, so I thought it would be better to just leave with no one the wiser."

"I can't believe Lexie never told me. In all these years. Or your father, for that matter."

"I swore them both to secrecy."

"Well, whatever happened between you and Rance back then, you were both kids. You're adults now. You're both responsible, and y'all love that little girl. I hope you'll do what's best for her. I think y'all would make a beautiful family."

"Stella." Larae set down her glass. "I won't marry him just to make Jayda happy. There's so much baggage. He probably resents me for not telling him. I still don't know if I can trust him for the long haul. And his stupid bull got out and tried to pulverize us yesterday. Jayda's traumatized and couldn't sleep alone."

"Bulls get out, Larae. Your bulls have gotten out. This is Texas. It happens. That doesn't make Rance irresponsible." Stella pointed a fork at her. "Now, you know I try to stay out of your business. But he slept in the guest room to make Jayda feel secure. That's a good daddy. And a good daddy makes a good husband. So in my book, that makes him a keeper."

"I forgot my keys." Rance stepped in the kitchen.

And heat promptly crept over Larae's face. Had he heard anything?

"What?" He splayed his hands.

Maybe not. Or he could be playing innocent.

"Just girl talk." Stella set her plate in the sink. "You weren't eavesdropping now, were you?"

"I wasn't dropping no eaves," he paraphrased from *Lord of the Rings* as he nabbed his keys from the counter. "I actually walked all the way home before I realized I'd left my keys here."

Maybe he hadn't heard anything.

"Let's try this again," he said, and walked out.

Stella gave Larae a shrug as Jayda skipped back into the room.

"I'm ready, Mommy."

"Then let's get to it."

Outside, the crew was installing the bleachers, while Jayda helped Larae organize the concession stand. The stand had come equipped with a small cold buffet for lettuce, tomatoes, pickles and onions lining the space beside the grill on the back wall, with a refrigerator and storage for buns, condiments and nachos to the side.

She could have gotten a freezer with it, as well, but she'd wanted smaller than the company offered. Since she already had a large freezer in the garage, she could store excess food there and have more available space in the stand.

With sliding windows on the front for taking orders and money, plus some on the side for selling rodeo tickets and registering contestants, the concession stand would be a multitasking hub, with the bathrooms behind it. Larae had already decided she'd work there to save money.

"Can I work in the 'cession stand, Mommy?"

"Concession stand. You can help me. You can definitely be the designated fly swatter since you're good at that."

"The windows are all glassed in. We won't have any flies."

"Trust me, every time we open the windows to take money or pass food out, they'll make a beeline to get in."

"Excuse me, miss. I'll take two cheeseburgers with the works." Rance grinned at them from the front window.

"You'll have to come back next weekend, mister." Jayda giggled. "Are you gonna work the concession stand with us, Daddy?"

"Oh no, Pumpkin." Larae's heart skipped a beat. "That's too much to ask. I'll hire someone to work with me."

"There's no need for that. I can help out. Save you some money." He disappeared around the side, opened the door and stepped inside the stand. "We'll make it a family operation."

Except they weren't really a family. And the stand suddenly seemed entirely too small with him in it, as if he sucked all the oxygen out of the space with his mere presence.

"Let's do it, Daddy. It'll be all kinds of fun."

Not the exact words Larae had in mind. More like torment. "You really don't have to do that. You're my stock contractor, and you've already gone above and beyond."

"I want to do it. It'll be fun working with Baby Girl, here. And if your rodeo is successful, that makes me successful."

There was just no way to get rid of him. And the worst part was that she didn't want to get rid of him. How had this happened? Despite all her defenses, Rance Shepherd had wormed himself into her heart all over again. Had he ever actually left it?

"You got any burgers fried up?" Denny popped his head through the side window.

"I'm sorry, mister, but the rodeo isn't until next weekend. We're just in here getting ready." Jayda giggled.

"Oh, well in that case, I got all my morning chores done, and there's a pinto pony that needs somebody to ride her. Any takers?"

"Me! Me! Me!" Jayda raised her hand, jumping up and down.

"Well, come on then. Time's a-wasting."

Jayda scampered out the door.

"Thanks, Denny," Larae said, although his timing was off, leaving her alone with Rance.

"No problem." He tipped his hat and ambled off after Jayda.

"I really can handle this, if you have something else to do." Her gaze caught Rance's, then flicked away before she could drown in those eyes.

"Nothing better to do. I'm just glad she seems okay and didn't have any more nightmares. What can I do to help?"

Go away. And stay away. "Chris sent the menu sign over. I'm impressed. He's fast and accurate, just like you said. We can put it up." She handed it to him.

"Just hamburgers, hot dogs, nachos and sunflower seeds. No fries or onion rings?"

"In my experience, those are the items that sell. We might try a bigger variety once we're indoors, but that's it for now."

"Where do you want it?"

"Let me go out and help you center it on the beam over the grill."

"See, you do need me." He shot her a wink.

Her face scalded as she turned away and stepped outside. "That's debatable. But whatever." By the time she got to the front, her cheeks felt normal. "Hold it up higher. Higher. Higher. Right there."

"You sure it's not too high? We don't want customers having to crane their necks."

"It's high enough that the workers won't obstruct the view, but I can read it without tilting my head back."

"All right then, if you'll hold it, I'll put it up. Got a hammer and nails handy?"

She hurried back inside and reached as high as she could to hold the sign in place. "Tools are right behind you on the counter. There's even a level so you can make sure it's straight."

"I forgot what a perfectionist you are. And you're a shorty." He snickered.

"I prefer the term *petite*."

"Whatever." He grinned and tapped a nail into one corner of the board before crossing to the other corner in front of her.

Too close. All her nerve endings went on alert. Why hadn't she turned her back to him instead of facing him?

"That looks just about right." He tapped the second nail in place, and his gaze dropped to hers.

She let go of the sign and tried to step back, but there wasn't anywhere to go.

Only inches separated them, and his gaze dropped to her lips. Her breath hushed as his head dipped.

"Is Larae in there?" Stella asked.

Rance jerked back and spun around.

"Sorry to interrupt." Stella stood at the front window, and her gaze pinged back and forth between them. "Now, don't freak out. I think she's okay. Except for maybe her arm."

Larae bolted out the door and headed for the barn. There was a circle of ranch hands in the barnyard. Beans was standing with no rider. "Oh, dear God"—she glanced Heavenward "—please let her be all right."

Rance passed her and got there first. The men allowed him access.

By the time Larae caught up, Rance was kneeling beside a crying Jayda.

"It hurts, Daddy." Her right wrist hung at an odd angle as she held it up with her other hand.

Nausea hit Larae, and she swallowed hard.

"I know, Baby Girl."

"Can you move it, sweetie?" Larae knelt on her other side.

Jayda shook her head then hiccuped a sob.

"I'm pretty sure it's broken." Rance winced. "I'm going

to pick you up, Baby Girl, and we'll get you to Urgent Care. Does anything else hurt?"

"No!" Jayda wailed.

"Let me stabilize it." Denny pushed through the crowd of hands and slipped a small board under her wrist and hand. "Lay it down now, Little Miss."

"It'll hurt."

"I know, but it'll help keep your bones lined up, and that'll help the doctor fix it where it won't hurt so much."

With trusting, tear-filled eyes, Jayda let Denny lay her injured arm on the board. She grimaced, and more tears came as he put a soft towel over her arm. Then he wound a strip of baling twine loosely to secure the board and tied it in place. "That'll keep it from flopping around till you see the doc."

"I know it hurts, Pumpkin. But the doctor will make it all better."

Rance picked her up gently while Larae supported the board, and they tag-teamed it to her SUV. Larae opened the door to the back seat and slid across while holding Jayda's injured arm steady. Rance set her inside, jumped into the drivers' seat and peeled out as Jayda whimpered against Larae.

"It's gonna be okay, sweetie. Just a few more minutes and we'll be there."

But it seemed like an hour had passed, and they'd barely pulled out of the driveway.

Chapter Fifteen

Rance was driving entirely too fast, but a vise grip tightened around his heart with each one of Jayda's cries. He pulled into the urgent care clinic, jumped out and swung the back door open.

"Easy, let me hold her arm while you get her out." Larae slid across the seat as he gently picked up Jayda.

With a whimper, she clung to him with her good arm and buried her face in his neck, while Larae supported her injured arm. They made slow progress across the parking lot, as if they were in a potato sack race with too many limbs not in unison.

Larae opened the door and backed inside, and they made it to the front desk. "She fell off her pony. I think her arm is broken."

"Name please." The nurse smiled reassuringly. Larae gave the pertinent information, and the nurse handed her a clipboard. "Fill this out. Once you get the first two forms finished, give them to me, and I'll get her logged in while you finish."

"Thank you." Rance managed, even though he wanted to barrel through the doors and shout until a doctor came running. He sat down without jarring Jayda and took the injured arm from Larae so she could get busy on the paperwork.

"It hurts, Daddy," Jayda whimpered.

"I know, Baby Girl. We'll see the doctor real soon, and he'll make it all better." He hoped. What if she ended up needing surgery? *Lord, please let it be a clean break.*

"I saw a bull by the arena in the back pasture and I got scared, so I got Beans to run the other way, but I didn't have a good hold of the reins, so I lost them and fell off. It wasn't Beans's fault. It was the bull that made me fall."

His eyes met Larae's over the top of Jayda's head.

"Pumpkin, we don't have any mean bulls. He wouldn't have bothered you."

"I don't like bulls, Mommy. Can we get rid of him?"

"We'll figure something out to make sure you feel safe." Rance ran his hand over her back in soothing circles as he scanned the rest of the people in the waiting room. All adults, no blood. Hopefully, they'd get Jayda in soon.

Larae finished the second sheet and turned it in to the nurse.

Before she got back to her seat, the door opened. "Jayda Collins."

Rance stood.

"I can get her wrist." Larae stuck the remaining forms under her arm.

"I've got her." He followed the nurse down a hall with doors on each side.

She escorted them into a room. "If you know her height and weight, we won't have to get it."

Not a clue.

Larae supplied the info.

"And she's seven?" A hint of surprise sounded in the nurse's tone.

"Yes, I was always small for my age, too."

"And you're her mother?"

"Yes."

"I'm her dad."

The nurse barely acknowledged him as she typed

something on the laptop and asked a few more questions he didn't know the answers to.

Maybe he was insignificant when it came to Jayda. He'd have to be sure and change that.

"I'll check with the doctor on ibuprofen for the pain, and he'll be with you shortly."

Jayda's whimpers had turned into a steady stream, and Rance's heart was about to burst as Larae finished filling out the paperwork.

The door opened, and a baby-faced man wearing a white lab coat stepped inside. "I'm Dr. Prewitt. Who do we have here?"

"This is our daughter, Jayda. We think her arm is broken."

"How old are you, Jayda?"

"Seven." She sniffled, her face still hidden in Rance's neck.

"Can I take a look at that arm?"

She shook her head.

"He can't fix it if we don't let him look at it." Larae gently coaxed. "Turn around so he can get to it."

Rance turned her around to face the doctor, supporting her arm as he did so.

"That's some splint you got there. Is your daddy a doctor, too?"

"Our ranch foreman did that." Rance was ready for this guy to do something. "Can she have something for the pain?"

"The nurse is bringing ibuprofen. Maybe your ranch foreman should become a doctor. I need to take it off, but I'll be real easy with it while your daddy holds your arm straight for me."

Rance held her hand and her elbow while Dr. Prewitt unwound the bailing wire and gently pulled off the towel and board.

The doctor cupped her wrist in both hands, feeling

around with his fingers. "It looks and feels like you broke your radius. That's the large bone in your wrist. We'll need to x-ray to make sure. What happened?"

"I fell off Beans." Jayda sobbed.

"A pony."

The door opened, and a nurse stepped inside. "Ibuprofen for Jayda Collins."

"Thank you." Larae took the plastic cup of pink medicine and handed the nurse the completed forms before turning her attention back to Jayda. "Here, sweetie. This will make it stop hurting." She helped Jayda sip until the liquid was all gone.

"It feels like a clean break, so if that's the case, I'll be able to set it without surgery. We'll know for sure once I get an X-ray. The nurse will show you the way, and you can carry Jayda there." The doctor gave them a reassuring grin. "You're being awfully brave, Jayda. Just a little longer."

"This way." The nurse hurried out of the room, with Rance and Larae following.

Once in the X-ray room, Jayda kept her face buried in Rance's chest while the technician gently laid her wrist on the machine, took a picture, repositioned it and took another.

The nurse met them in the hall with a cheery smile. "All done. I'll take you back to the exam room now."

Jayda didn't seem to be crying as hard now. Maybe the ibuprofen was kicking in.

They each settled into chairs with Jayda sideways in Rance's lap, leaning into him.

"Is it feeling better, Pumpkin?"

"A little."

The doctor strolled in and turned on the X-ray screen. "It's a clean radius break, right here." He pointed to a dark line on the screen. "I can set it today and cast it. Six weeks later, Jayda will be good as new."

"Is it gonna hurt?" Jayda whimpered.

"Can you give her something to deaden it?" Larae asked.

"Let me see." The doctor gently cupped Jayda's wrist in his hands and felt around with his thumbs, then did a quick little twist.

"Ow." Jayda wailed.

"Wait a minute." Rance tried to push the doctor's hands away.

"I just set it." The doctor placed her arm in her lap. "How does that feel, Jayda?"

"Better."

Rance could clobber the doctor for hurting her. But as her tears dried, the heat of his anger slowly seeped away.

"The nurse will put a cast on it. You can pick the color—pink, purple, anything you want. Keep it dry for six weeks, and we'll set up an appointment to take it off."

"You mean I can't swim?" Jayda's face puckered again.

"By the time it gets warm enough for that, your cast will history. In the meantime, if you go to an indoor pool, you can wrap it in a plastic bag and keep your arm out of the water."

"Don't worry, Pumpkin. Time will fly by."

"What color cast do you want?"

"Pink."

"I'll tell the nurse."

"Thank you, Dr. Prewitt." Larae smiled as he hurried out of the room.

The nurse returned with a roll of pink fiberglass casting. She slipped Jayda's arm into a soft sleeve, then began wrapping her arm from between her thumb and index finger up to a few inches from her elbow.

"Who do you want to sign your cast first?" The nurse finished her task.

"Daddy."

His heart warmed, until he saw the hurt in Larae's eyes.

"A daddy's girl, huh?" The nurse gave them a few more instructions on keeping the cast clean and dry, then said they could go.

"You okay, Baby Girl?" Rance stood and tucked her close.

"It doesn't hurt near as much as it did."

"Your bones are lined up now, and the medicine has probably kicked in." Larae patted her back, looking like an outsider with her nose pressed to the glass. "Let's go home."

He had to do something to include Larae.

They walked out of the clinic, shrouded in silence all the way to the SUV.

"You can sit in the back with Mommy." Maybe that would fix it.

"No." Jayda clung to him tighter.

He couldn't bring himself to look at Larae. "Listen, Baby Girl. Now that I know about you, I'm not going anywhere. We've got the rest of our lives to be together. But you can't forget your mama. She took care of you all these years by herself, and she's worried about you, too."

"I'm sorry, Mommy."

He chanced a glance at Larae and glimpsed her glossy eyes as she ducked into the back seat. He set Jayda down beside her, and Larae helped her into her car seat. Once she was all snapped in, she leaned her head against Jayda's.

Tread carefully. He couldn't oust Larae while he bonded with Jayda. Larae would never forgive him. And she already had enough to forgive him for.

Despite her broken wrist, Jayda insisted on going to church the next day. But Larae did convince her they shouldn't go to class just yet with a promise they'd attend next week.

Jayda's cast had received a lot of attention and signatures, and Larae felt just as at home and peaceful as she had the week before.

As soon as the sermon was over, Rance hurried them to the lobby. They shook the pastor's hand and exited as Rance ushered them across the parking lot.

Why was he in such a hurry? Was he worried Jayda's arm might start hurting?

"Larae Collins, is that you?"

Rance tugged her toward her SUV.

"Larae?"

"Wait, someone's calling my name."

He stopped and closed his eyes.

Larae frowned and turned around. Evangeline Chadwick hurried down the church steps toward her. Delia Rhinehart's cohort. Larae's jaw dropped. Dressed in discount department store clothing instead of Gucci.

"I thought that was you." She ducked her head. Unsure of herself?

This wasn't the Evangeline Larae knew at all. "Hello, Evangeline."

"Please, call me Angie."

Huh? Was she caught in the twilight zone?

"It's good to see you." Evangeline—Angie—smiled. "You have a sweet family."

"Oh, we're not."

"Mommy, can I go talk to Amelia?"

"I'll take her. Unless you need me to stick around." Rance offered a lifeline.

"No, we'll be fine."

He scooped Jayda up and ambled across the lot toward Amelia and her mom.

"But he is her father, right?"

Larae straightened her spine, ready for harsh words and judgment. "I'm a Christian now. I realize what I did back then was wrong. But I don't need salt rubbed in my guilt."

"Don't worry, dear. I'm not condemning you." Her gaze went to Jayda. "God can turn mistakes into blessings."

What? Encouragement? "How did you know?"

"I can tell by the way he is with her. I'm assuming you were pregnant when you left Medina all those years ago. And I suspect you left because of judgmental old biddies like I was."

Huh? Larae almost swallowed her tongue.

"I'm sorry for the way I used to be, if I ever made you feel less than. I'm not like that anymore." Evangeline— Angie—slipped her arm through Larae's, as if they were old friends.

"What happened?" The question slipped out.

"Well, after the whole tragedy with your poor dear mother and that nasty lie Delia told, I kept right on riding my high horse, looking down my nose at everyone, even Delia." She patted Larae's arm. "Until last year. When my husband traded me in for a new model. She's younger than our daughter."

"I'm so sorry." And she really was. No one deserved such treatment. Not even Angie.

"That knocked me right off the throne I'd created for myself. Suddenly, none of my so-called friends wanted anything to do with me. It was like I had a disease and they were afraid they'd catch it. Or their husbands would."

Poor Angie.

"I was raised middle-class and once my world with Reginald fell apart, I realized what money had done to me. I put almost everything I got in the divorce settlement in a trust for our daughter. I have an apartment in Fredericksburg, but I don't fit there anymore and I constantly run into reminders of my past. I'm looking at property in Medina and decided to attend church here this morning."

"I'm glad you're moving forward."

"I'm going to see Delia this weekend." Angie closed

her eyes. "She had a massive stroke not long after my marriage busted up, and she's been in the nursing home since."

"Oh, my. I hadn't heard."

"No one ever comes to see her. Not her husband or even her children. The poor dear is wasting away in a wheelchair, unable to communicate. I've told her all about turning over my new leaf, and it seemed like there was something in her eyes. I think she wishes she could do the same. You wouldn't want to come with me to see her, would you?"

"No." Larae shook her head. "I can't."

"I understand." Angie patted her arm again. "I hope you can forgive me for every mean, rotten, tainted thing that ever came out of my mouth."

"Yes." The word slipped out. "I can."

"It's good to see you, dear. I hope you and Rance work things out. Or you find what you need elsewhere."

"Thank you."

Angie hugged her, then walked away. Alone.

Larae strolled over to where Rance waited on a bench while Jayda and Amelia made wildflower necklaces.

"She seemed different."

"Very."

"I almost didn't recognize her. When I did, I tried to spare you."

"It was actually good to see her." Larae filled him on everything Angie had faced. "I can't remember her daughter's name. Can you?"

He closed his eyes. "Regina."

"That's it. I wonder if they have a good relationship. I hope so. She seemed so alone."

"Who'd have thought you'd feel sorry for Evangeline Chadwick."

"Really." She took in a deep breath and shared the part about Delia. "I don't think I can go to see her."

"Understandable."

A ball of anger clenched her heart, as it had since her mom died. She knew she needed to let it go, to forgive Delia. But how could she forgive the woman who'd made her mom's coma and death even harder?

"Now I'm not trying to pressure you. But, if you get to thinking on it and you want to go, I'll go with you."

The sweetness of his offer wound around her heart. "Don't hold your breath." She stood. "Come on, Jayda. You're supposed to rest that arm."

"Where's your mama, Amelia?" Rance set his Stetson in place.

"Over there talking to your mama."

He ruffled Amelia's hair. "I told her I'd watch you, but I'm leaving, so scurry on over there where she is now."

"Bye, Jayda. I'll see you at school tomorrow." Amelia skipped over to her mom.

"Will I be able to go to school, Mommy?"

"The doctor said as long as you're not hurting and you skip recess."

They piled into the SUV, with Larae deep in thought. If Evangeline Chadwick could change into Angie, could Rance change, too? He seemed less and less like the guy she had known in high school. More like a man she could depend on. And, more importantly, someone Jayda could count on.

Chapter Sixteen

Thirty minutes before his parents were to arrive to take Jayda to school, Rance found Larae and Jayda in their regular spots—this time watching the arena guys spread dirt as a crew worked on constructing the announcer's booth.

"Looking good."

Larae jumped and spun around. "You're always sneaking up on us. I should be used to it by now."

"Daddy!" Jayda ran to him despite her hot pink cast, then cocked her head toward the arena. "This is just the first layer. Did you know there are three layers in a good arena floor? What are they, Mommy?"

"Each is a special mixture of sand or silt or loam."

"Those things. Mommy knows all about arenas."

"She sure does. I want y'all to come over to my place for a minute."

"Why?" Larae checked her watch. "Your parents will be here any minute."

"Is the bull over there?" Jayda pursed her lips.

"That's what I want to show you. I had my wood fences replaced with steel rails where I keep the bulls. I want to show you they can't get out, so you don't have to be scared."

"I don't want to go." Jayda shook her head.

"And you know what?" Larae shot him a glare. "You don't have to."

"I just think since you live here, you should be able to have a picnic or ride Beans wherever you want and not be afraid. Sometimes facing your fears can make them go away. And seeing my new pens will help you realize there's nothing to fear from the bulls. They're not going anywhere anymore."

"You promise?"

"I promise."

Jayda's mouth twitched as she thought it over. "Okay, 'cause I don't like being scared."

Larae's steady glare turned to steel.

He ignored her and scooped Jayda up, then turned toward the long driveway.

A heavy sigh sounded behind him and the gravel crunched as Larae hurried to catch up.

"You don't have to come."

"If you insist on terrorizing her, I'm coming along."

"I'm trying to help." His words came out harsher than he'd intended.

"Daddy, are you mad at Mommy?"

"No, Baby Girl." Just frustrated.

"Sometimes Mommy and Daddy won't agree on what's best for you." Larae practically jogged to keep up with him. "But that doesn't mean we're mad."

He slowed his stride so she didn't have to work so hard as they neared the side gate to his place.

"Can we stop here, Daddy? Just show me from here."

He stopped. "I won't force you, but you really can't see anything from here. I wasn't planning on taking you all the way to the fence, just far enough for you to see the bulls won't get out."

"Okay, Daddy. I trust you."

His heart turned to butter. If only her mother could do the same.

He unlatched the gate, stepped into his yard, then continued around the side of the house. With Larae right

on his heels. At the back of the house, he stopped. Still
a hundred yards away from the steel fence, they had a
clear view of the massive creatures as they ate from their
troughs. He looked down at Jayda.

Her eyes were squeezed closed, and she clung to him
with all her might.

"Take a look."

"I'm scared, Daddy."

"We're a long way away. I just want you to look. We
won't go any closer."

"You don't have to, sweetie." Larae put her hand on
Jayda's back. "We can go home right now if you want."

"I don't like being scared." Jayda opened her eyes.

Just then one of the bulls tussled with another and
rammed into the steel rail.

She tightened her grip on him.

"See how the fence didn't even shake?"

"Uh-huh."

"They can't get out, Baby Girl. I promise. None of
my bulls will ever chase you again. Do you believe me?"

The bull that had chased them clashed with another
and crashed into the rail.

"I like your new fence, Daddy."

"I'm glad. You're a very brave little girl. How about
we meet Grandma and Grandpa at the end of the driveway. They'll be along any minute."

"Okay."

They retraced their steps and had barely gotten back
to Larae's drive when his folks pulled in.

His father stopped beside them and rolled down his
window. "What are y'all doing?"

"Just showing Jayda my new fence."

"The bulls can't get out anymore." Jayda pushed at
him to let her down.

"That's a really good thing." His mom leaned forward
to see them.

He set Jayda down, and she gave Larae a hug, then crawled into the car. "See you after school."

"Bye, Daddy. Bye, Mommy."

They waved until the car disappeared, then headed back toward Larae's house.

"As much as I hate to admit it, you were right. She needed to see that the bulls were secure."

"I might be getting the hang of this dad thing."

"Maybe." She peered up at him, then looked away.

They walked the rest of the way in companionable silence. Could they get the hang of doing this parenting thing together?

He heard a massive engine and air brakes behind them. Rance turned to see an 18-wheeler pull into the drive. They stepped to the side to let it pass.

"Maybe the concession stand food."

"I hope you're wrong." Larae covered her face with her hands. "I need a freezer first."

"We better go see."

What else could go wrong? With the bull episode and Jayda's arm, the more Rance hung around, the more he realized she needed help. Needed him. Even if she'd never admit it.

"It's almost noon." Larae propped her hands on her hips. "What am I supposed to do with all this food? And no freezer?"

Rance scanned the pallet full of boxes. "Don't panic. The freezer is supposed to come today."

"And it's not hot out here." Denny leaned against the boxes. "The food is frozen, so it should be fine."

"I'm calling the company. It should have been here by now." She scrolled through her contacts and selected the number.

It rang several times, and a perky woman greeted her on speakerphone.

"Yes, I ordered a freezer, and it was supposed to be here first thing this morning. Can you check on my order for Collins Ranch in Medina?"

"Sure, let me pull up your account. Let's see, I show that the driver delivered your freezer three hours ago."

"But that can't be. It's not here."

A small gasp sounded over the phone.

"What?"

"I'm afraid your freezer is in Medina—Ohio."

"Oh, no."

"I didn't know there was another one anywhere else." Rance scoffed.

"I'm so sorry, ma'am. Apparently someone keyed the order in wrong."

"When can I get a freezer? I need it today."

"Let me check. Looks like I'll have another driver available tomorrow."

Larae squeezed her eyes closed, trying to rein in her frustration and remain polite. "My food won't last until then."

"I'm so sorry, ma'am. I can check with my supervisor and see if there's anything else we can do. Maybe a discount for your trouble?"

"Do you have any other freezers like the one I ordered in stock? And can you please actually check what you have on the floor and not just your computer?"

"Yes ma'am. Please hold."

"I can't believe this." She rolled her eyes. "If they have one, I'm going to get it."

"I can go get it for you," Denny offered.

"I can handle it. But thanks."

"We can take my truck." Rance adjusted his hat. "We never put the grand opening flyers out in San Antonio, so we can do that too and be back by four or five."

"Ma'am." The clerk came back on the line. "We have two in our showroom."

"You're positive?"

"Yes, ma'am, I personally checked the model number on both units. We have two."

"Okay, I want my name on one of them. I'm coming to get it."

"I already marked it for you and removed it from inventory in the computer."

"Thank you. I'll see you in a few hours." Larae ended the call. "I'll put the flyers out before I pick up the freezer."

"Let's get cracking." Rance headed for his truck.

"You don't have to go. I can take Dad's truck."

"We can get the flyers out quicker if we tag-team it. And I want to make sure the freezer gets strapped down so we don't lose it on the interstate."

"If we're not back until four or five, I think the food needs to be put somewhere. Some of it can go in the garage freezer like I planned. You need to stay here and handle that."

"The hands and I can tackle it, Larae. Y'all go." Denny waved his hand toward Rance's truck. "I don't want you hauling a freezer home by yourself. Now git."

Larae hesitated. Why did she always get stuck with him? With no other option, she stalked toward his truck.

"Well, you sure are good for my ego."

"Just hush and drive." Larae opened the passenger door and climbed up as if she was going before the firing squad. "I'll call your folks and let them know what's going on."

"They'll be tickled to get extra Jayda time."

"I was actually looking forward to that myself." She sighed. "I wanted to be here so I could go get her if her arm starts hurting."

"The doctor said she'd be fine. But if not, Mom and Dad can fetch her early."

She dialed the number. While it rang, she admitted to

herself that despite all her protests, there was a part of her that didn't mind spending time with this new and improved version of Rance.

Chapter Seventeen

Why had Rance pounced on the opportunity to spend uninterrupted hours alone with her when she still considered him to be the jerk who dumped her in high school? When she obviously wanted nothing to do with him? And how would he get over her if he kept spending day after day at her side?

By eating on the road, they got the flyers posted and had picked up the freezer by three. They headed home.

Rance checked his mirrors, merged into the right lane and took the exit to the interstate. "Well, you got a nice discount for your trouble."

"True, but I'd rather have had the freezer this morning."

And avoided the trip with him. He was getting good at reading between her lines. "Let me know if you need to stop for anything?"

She gave him a determined shake of her head. "I want to get home to Jayda. That bull terrorized her just last week, and it's been two days since she broke her arm. I hated being away from her today."

"I wish I'd thought to hide her face instead of letting her watch the bull the whole time. Poor kid."

"You saved her. We can deal with the bad memories. I couldn't deal with it if anything had happened to her."

"Me, neither."

A truck sped up beside him then cut in front of him.

"Whoa!" Larae put her hands on the dash, bracing for impact.

Rance's heart vaulted as he checked his mirror. There was a car right on his tail and traffic on each side of them.

The car zoomed into the next lane and took an exit.

"That was close." He loosened his grip on the steering wheel. "Guess he almost missed his exit."

"If he'd hit us, we'd have been in an instant pileup. People are crazy. Why do they never realize they can always turn around or find another route?"

"We're all right though." But what if they hadn't been? There'd been an 18-wheeler on their right. Larae would have been toast. The thought put an ache in his heart.

And where would that have left Jayda?

"Not to be morbid or anything, but do you have any arrangements for Jayda if anything happens to you?"

"Hoping I'll die so you can have her?" she snapped.

"Absolutely not," he growled. "But if I'd jerked the wheel, that 18-wheeler would have—" He couldn't finish the sentence. "It got me thinking."

"I'm way ahead of you. After my dad got sick, I made arrangements for Lexie to take her."

"A good choice. But now that I'm in the picture, I'd like that changed."

"We'll see."

"There's no 'we'll see' about it, Larae." He gripped the steering wheel tighter again. "Am I even listed as her father on her birth certificate?"

"Yes."

"Then legally, I'd get her."

"My lawyer wrote up papers saying that since you'd had no contact with her and since Lexie has been in her life, my wishes are for Lexie to get custody."

His chest burned. "I didn't have any contact with her because you didn't tell me about her."

Silence.

"You didn't tell your lawyer that little nugget, did you?"

"Not exactly."

"Please get it changed, Larae. She's my daughter."

"You really think you could raise her on your own?" She blew out a frustrated sigh. "Because I remember this guy who went from girl to girl to girl, and I'm having a hard time with leaving my child in that guy's care."

"I'm not that guy anymore." Would she ever see anything other than the worst in him? "Surely you realize that."

"I'm trying. But I still expect you to pick up and leave or chase some skirt anytime. And leave Jayda in your wake."

"There hasn't been anyone in my life for five years, Larae. Five years." He passed an 18-wheeler and crossed to the slow lane again. "And the few between you and the last five years weren't anything serious. I'm not going anywhere. Why can't you just believe me?"

"Because I believed every pretty little word you whispered in my ear back in high school, and I ended up pregnant and alone."

And he couldn't tell her why. "Don't you realize that if I'd known you were carrying my child, you wouldn't have been alone?"

"I didn't want you to marry me out of duty. You'd have ended up resenting me." She squeezed her eyes closed. "But you probably do anyway because I kept her a secret."

"I guess you did what you thought was right for Jayda."

"I'll get the papers changed. But can I leave her to your parents instead of you?"

"Seriously?"

"No. But I'd feel better about it."

"Well, nothing's going to happen to you, so none of this will even matter. It just matters to my heart. I want to know Jayda will always have at least one parent to love her."

"And that's all I want."

He covered her hand with his. "Finally, we agree on something."

Why did they always have to take two steps forward and one step back? But she didn't move her hand. It felt really nice. And did funny things to his pulse.

While the crew worked into the afternoon on the corral and a maze of pens, Larae leaned on the arena fence. Would this thing come together in three more days? Friday night, she was supposed to host her first rodeo. While the arena, concession stand, announcer's booth and bleachers were ready, building pens would take two days, and the old entry and exit chutes still had to be updated. Plus, the parking area needed a load of gravel.

She probably should have put off her grand opening for at least a week, but the ranch was still bleeding red. She was determined to turn a profit as soon as possible.

When they'd gotten home last night, Rance had helped her round up all the hamburgers and hot dogs Stella and Denny had stored in employees' freezers, while the hands had unloaded the new freezer and maneuvered it into the concession stand. There was no way she could have gotten this far by herself. Her employees had been invaluable. And so had Rance. She just hated admitting it.

The heat of a blush swept over her at the memory of his hand on hers in the truck yesterday. Why hadn't she moved?

Heavy equipment swirled dust around the foundation of the indoor arena with construction beginning. Was she crazy to go ahead with the building? Should she wait and make sure the outdoor arena was a success before going ahead with the project? Too late now.

Yet, with her ranch hanging by a thread, Rance inserting himself deeper into her life daily and Jayda sporting a neon pink cast, the most pressing thing on her mind was Delia Rhinehart.

Why could she not get the conversation with Angie out of her mind?

"What should I do, Lord?" More than anything, she did not want to see Delia Rhinehart. "Maybe I could write her a letter."

Peace threaded through her.

A deep sigh seeped out of her. "I guess I'll take that as a yes."

"I don't think they can hear you." Rance shouted above the noise.

"Why must you always sneak up on me?" She swung around. "I wasn't talking to them. I was praying. Sort of."

"I can't help it if you're always standing with your back to me. I'm glad you and God are on speaking terms, though."

"Me, too." She turned back toward the arena.

He took up residence at the fence beside her.

"Think it'll get done in time?" she said.

"I do."

"How come you're so confident?"

"Because we're both praying about it."

"That's not exactly what I was praying about. I mean I have. But not just now." She drew in a deep breath. "I need to forgive Delia Rhinehart. To write her a letter saying that I do. For now. And maybe eventually go see her."

"That's—"

"Crazy?"

"Intense."

"I haven't been able to get her off my mind since we saw Angie."

"I could take you?"

"I'm not ready to see her. I've got the rodeo. My first weekend."

"Does it have to be the weekend?"

"I'm not sure. That's when Angie said she was going."

"What nursing home is it?"

Larae gave him the name, then tilted her head back and did a neck roll from side to side. Numerous pops and cracks sounded. What she wouldn't give for a good shoulder massage.

Rance scrolled through his phone. "It doesn't say on the website, but maybe you and Angie could go together sometime. That way you wouldn't be alone. I could drive you."

"Maybe I'll be ready someday, but I don't know how to get in touch with Angie anyway."

"She might be at church tomorrow night. And if she's not, I can ask around, or we can call and check with the nursing home."

"To be honest, I'm not sure what I'd do if I went. Or even what to write in a letter. Yell and scream at her. Or forgive her."

"You'll do the right thing."

"How can you be so sure?"

"Because I know you. And you know Jesus." He stepped behind her, and his hands settled on her shoulders.

She stiffened.

"Relax." His fingers kneaded the sore muscles in her shoulders. "All your stress still goes to your neck and shoulders."

In spite of herself, she turned to pudding as his thumbs worked out her kinks.

Gravel crunched under tires behind them, and his hands fell away as they turned around. Maggie and Davis were bringing Jayda home.

As soon as the car stopped rolling, the back door flew

open and Jayda popped out. She aimed herself toward them at a dead run.

"Slow down, sweetie. You don't want to fall."

But Jayda kept running. "Look at my cast. Everybody in my class has signed it now. Plus my teacher." She finally stopped as they reached her.

"Did your arm hurt today?" Rance asked.

"Uh-uh." Jayda shook her head. "Look."

They both knelt as she showed them the signatures most important to her and explained who each child was. When she finished, she hurled herself at them for a group hug.

"Whoa." In trying to steady Jayda, Rance lost his balance and bumped into Larae.

They landed sprawled beside each other with Jayda on top of him.

"Sorry, Daddy." Jayda giggled.

"Is everybody okay?" Davis called.

"All except for my pride." Larae laughed. "Thanks for bringing her home."

"Be careful with that cast, Baby Girl. That thing's a weapon."

"She hit you with it?" Larae rolled onto her side to look him over.

"Just my chin."

"It's a wonder you didn't knock Daddy out."

His green eyes warmed at her calling him that.

"Lie down, Mommy. Let's watch the clouds." Jayda's innocent request tugged at her heart.

They'd never been able to see the clouds very well in the city. Larae lay on her back, mostly to escape Rance's gaze. Jayda flopped over, careful not to hit her, lying half on Rance and half on Larae.

"We'll see you tomorrow," Maggie called from the car window.

The car engine faded down the driveway, leaving

them to this perfect moment. With Rance by her side and Jayda's weight on her chest, Larae could live forever in this moment. With the man she loved by her side, cuddling with the child of their hearts. Could he be a permanent fixture in their lives? Could they be a family—the way it should be—forever?

Between them, the back of his hand rested against hers. He moved his arm enough to thread his fingers through hers.

She stiffened, and then, of their own volition, her fingers tightened around his. He turned to look at her. She met his gaze, and fireworks went off in her heart. Eyes she could drown in. He'd done nothing but support her since she'd been back. With Jayda, with the rodeo and with her Delia dilemma.

Maybe, just maybe, she wasn't as completely opposed to trying again with him as she'd been a few weeks ago.

But could they stop arguing all the time? And could she trust him to stick around on a permanent basis?

Chapter Eighteen

Two days remained until the rodeo's grand opening, and the pens were all in place as the crew pulled out of the drive. He'd tried to get a moment alone with Larae all day, but it seemed as if she was avoiding him. Now she'd disappeared.

Had he been wrong? Hadn't they had a moment yesterday, lying in the grass with their daughter, hands clasped and eyes locked? If Jayda hadn't been there, he'd have kissed her.

Once Jayda came home from school, she'd have to surface. But then they'd be consumed with Jayda. He strolled past the barn and heard soft humming.

He stopped and gingerly approached the open galley door, careful to walk softly. A figure stood at the last stall, face pressed against a horse's muzzle, highlighted by the light outside. Larae. His breath caught at her beauty, at the love she obviously felt for her horse. He was almost jealous of the big buckskin.

"Want to take her for a ride?"

She jumped, her standard response to him.

"Sorry, but for the record, I didn't come up behind you." He held his hands up in surrender.

"I wish. But I don't have time for a ride."

"Sure you do. The guys are done for the day." As his eyes adjusted to the dim lighting, he checked his watch.

"School's just getting out, but we've still got an hour before Mom and Dad bring Jayda home. And when she gets home, she can ride Beans with us."

"We should call them to let them know I'm done for the day and they should bring her straight home. She could ride with us now."

"We could. But you've been nonstop mom for seven years. All by yourself." He kept his tone light, no hint of accusation. "On top of that, you took care of your dad all those months after he moved in with you in Dallas. And you've been a frenzied rodeo organizer for almost three weeks. When's the last time you completely relaxed?"

She sagged against the horse. "I can't even remember."

"Saddle Molly up. We both need some fresh air."

"You remember her name."

"I remember everything that has to do with you, Larae." He strolled into the galley between the stalls. "Which one can I take?"

"The bay on your left."

He shot her a playful grin. "You're not setting me up with the wildest one you've got just so you can watch me land on my backside, are you?"

One eyebrow lifted. "Guess you'll have to see."

"Challenge accepted."

"There should be a saddle and gear in his stall."

"Hey, big guy." Rance stroked the horse's russet muzzle as he entered the stall. "How about a ride?" The horse stayed calm and still as Rance set a blanket on his broad back, then strapped on the saddle and slipped the halter into place around the ears and dark mane, and finally the bridle. "You're just a big softie, aren't you?"

As he led the horse from the stall, Larae was already astride Molly and waiting for him.

"What's his name?"

"Lancelot. He was Dad's."

Their eyes locked. That she'd let him ride her dad's horse had to mean something. Didn't it?

"He hasn't been ridden since Dad got sick, so I figure it's time."

And she busted his bubble. She was getting so good at that.

They rode side by side out of the barn.

"Race ya to the river." Her horse shot off ahead of him.

"Hey." He coaxed Lancelot into a gallop. "What happened to get ready, set, go?"

"You should always be ready." She shouted as her blond hair bounced in the wind behind her. She was a vision on her golden horse with its midnight mane and tail. "I win." She slowed Molly to a trot until he caught up.

"I think that was the most unfair race I've ever run."

Larae laughed and brought Molly to a halt at the water's edge.

They guided their horses into the river at a shallow point to cross.

"I wrote my letter to Delia last night."

"And?"

"I set out to rail at her for trying to ruin my mom's reputation. But when I started writing, it didn't come out that way. I forgave her—in the letter, and in my heart."

"I'm glad." He stopped beside her and reached for her hand. "It'll help you, more than it will her."

She stared at his outstretched fingers for a moment, then slipped her hand into his.

Maybe if she could forgive Delia, she could forgive him.

"Hear that?"

"What?" All he could hear was his overactive heart drumming in his ears.

"Silence."

They listened together for several minutes. But it

wasn't really silence. The songs and chirps of birds filled the air, along with a chorus of crickets.

"I've missed this."

"Me, too." But he meant her. He pointed in the distance. "I remember I was standing right over there."

"When?"

"When I saw you for the first time."

She blushed but didn't pull away.

"It was the summer I came to work for your dad before I transferred to private school. One of your daddy's cows had calved, and I was trying to get the calf back to the barn. The mama was fighting me, and I was having a hard time getting the baby up on my horse. I heard a noise and saw the blur of blond hair waving in the wind with Molly at full blast."

"I don't remember that."

"You didn't notice me. But I noticed you, riding like the wind. No fear. And after that one glimpse, I was determined to meet you."

"We better get back." She tugged her hand from his and turned Molly around toward the way they'd come. "Jayda will be home soon."

They trotted their horses back in silence, with him wondering what he'd said wrong.

"Aren't we taking her for a ride?"

"On second thought, I'm not sure it's a good idea with her arm in a cast."

They reached the barn. Inside, they worked at getting the gear off their respective horses in silence.

He was tired of silence.

At the same moment, they exited their stalls. She stopped. He didn't, stepping close to Larae and taking her hand in his.

"Listen, Larae. That pull we've always felt—it's still there. And I'm tired of ignoring it. To be honest, I'm not sure why we're ignoring it."

"Kiss her, Daddy." Jayda clapped her hands.

Larae sprang away from him. "Jayda, you're early."

"Uh-huh." Her grin stayed in place, as if she knew a secret.

"Where are Grandma and Grandpa?" Rance asked.

"On the porch. We saw y'all riding in, and they said I could come out to meet you."

"If we'd known you were early, we'd have come back sooner." Larae smoothed a hand over her hair.

"Or waited for you so you could ride with us." Rance shot Jayda a wink.

"It's okay." Her grin slipped away. "I don't want to ride. We came home early 'cause it's church night."

Rance caught Larae's gaze and a moment of understanding passed between them. Jayda was over her fear of bulls, but now she was afraid to ride.

"Want to go for a quick ride on my horse?" Rance motioned toward the porch. "Maybe Grandma and Grandpa will want to come, too. We've still got plenty of time before church."

"Nope. I don't want to." She looked down, then back up with a devious gleam in her eye. "If I'd gone with you, maybe you wouldn't have kissed Mommy."

Larae's face went crimson. "Daddy did not kiss me."

"Why not?"

"Because." She cleared her throat. "We don't have that kind of relationship."

"But I don't see why not. You've gotten to know each other again. Why don't y'all get married now?"

"It's complicated." Rance picked Jayda up. "Come ride with me. On my horse. That okay with you, Larae?"

"Yes."

At least she trusted him to keep Jayda safe, cast and all. That was something.

Jayda's blue eyes filled with trust. "Okay, Daddy. Let's see if Grandma and Grandpa want to go, too."

"You coming, Larae?"

"No. I have a few calls to make." She wouldn't look at him, eyes focused solely on Jayda. "But when you get back, I'll be done for the day, and we'll get ready for church."

"I wish you could come, too," Rance hinted.

"Me, too." Larae forced a smile. "But we'll go another day."

Despite her words, her thoughts reflected in her eyes. Spending another minute with him was the last thing she wanted.

And everything he longed for.

The chute slid down, then got hung up before lowering completely. It had been that way for a long time, but back when Larae used the arena to practice barrel racing, it hadn't mattered. She closed her eyes. Between the cloud of dust around the indoor arena's skeleton of steel framing and the truck pouring gravel over the parking lot, she almost needed a dust mask.

Last night, Angie had shown up at church again, and Larae had told her about mailing the letter and promised to pray about going to see Delia eventually. Maybe after the indoor arena was up and running, she'd have worked out the kinks and be better able to focus.

Right now, she had to concentrate on the rodeo. Tomorrow night, contestants, employees and attendees would converge. Whether they could get the chute working or not.

At least, she hoped she'd have attendees. They'd covered the area with flyers. She'd set up announcements on the radio, taken out newspaper ads, put information on the ranch website, and blasted social media. Hopefully, her marketing prowess would do the trick. She needed this thing to turn a profit, especially since construction on the indoor arena was in full swing.

"Try it now." Freddy, the ranch handyman, shouted.

From his perch on the fence, Rance lowered the chute. Slightly smoother, but it still had a catch to it. Maybe she should have let the construction crew work on it. But Freddy was certain he could fix it.

The entry gate to the arena was as smooth as silk. The bucking chutes were brand-new. The exit was the problem. And when the bullfighters corraled the bulls to the exit chute, it needed to close. Quick and secure. All this work, and something as simple as a gliding pulley system could derail her.

"Found it." Freddy held up a quarter-sized rock in his greasy fingers. "Now try."

She held her breath as Rance lowered the chute. The gate glided evenly, then hit the dirt with a thud.

"Like butter." Rance jumped down, loped toward her and threw his hat in the air. "*Yee-haw!* You know what that means?"

"What?"

"We're in business." He picked her up and twirled her around.

She couldn't breathe or think. Only feel. Every taut muscle. Every frantic beat of her heart. How could one man stir her emotions so? She felt completely protected and terrified at the same time.

He set her down.

She jerked away. "Don't ever do that again."

"Just a little celebration." He waggled his eyebrows at her. "I didn't mean to get you all worked up."

"Maybe you should find some bimbo to celebrate with. You're good at that." She stalked away.

"That was low, Larae." He matched her stride. "Surely, you must know by now I'm not like that anymore."

It was low. And she shouldn't have said it. Why did he consistently bring out the worst in her?

Because the way she felt for him terrified her. She'd

loved four people in her life. Her mom, her dad, Rance, and Jayda. Three out of the four times, she'd lost.

She stopped, and he kept going, then backtracked.

"Just because we have a daughter." She jabbed a finger at him. "That doesn't mean we're taking right back up where we started. This—" she waved her hand back and forth between them "—isn't happening. So stop with the memory lane, sweet-talking, want-to-kiss-me act. I fell for it once, but I won't again. You're in Jayda's life, not mine. Period. And we can't confuse her about our relationship. Understood?"

"I thought we were growing closer. Getting along."

"We're trying to get along for Jayda's sake. I appreciate all your help with the rodeo, but we're not growing closer. We're Jayda's parents. That's all."

"Okay." His gaze went to the gravel truck. "What about when Jayda gets home from school?"

"I don't think we need to spend so much time together, the three of us. It obviously confuses her and makes her want us to be a family. Maybe when your folks pick her up, you could spend a few hours with her at their house or at yours before y'all bring her home."

"I'll let them know." He scanned the arena. "Well, since everything's in working order here, I guess I'll see you tomorrow."

"I'll be busy making calls and setting up payroll, then going over details with my weekend employees when they arrive."

"Tomorrow night at the grand opening then?"

"Maybe." In passing only, she hoped.

"For what it's worth, you've done a great job of getting this thing organized in a very short time. I think it'll be a big success."

"Thanks. And I really do appreciate all your help."

He turned away, retrieved his hat and continued up her driveway.

Her heart thudded against her ribs. How had she allowed herself to fall for him all over again? He was the only man who'd ever had the power to crumble her heart. And she'd let him right back in.

Chapter Nineteen

With twenty minutes to spare, Rance waited as the last bull clambered out of his trailer and into the bucking chute.

"That's it for the first round." The young driver he'd hired to transport his bulls from next door secured the trailer gate. "I'll bring a fresh load before the second round."

"Thanks, Frankie. Good job."

Dressed in sparkles, Larae was out in the arena, with Jayda by her side, in a huddle of employees. Her outfit reminded him of when they'd been in high school and she'd been crowned the rodeo queen.

Oblivious to him, she conferred with the timers and chute boss he recognized from other rodeos. Also on hand were two bullfighters dressed in full clown gear and a couple of pickup men who had each gotten Rance out of a few scrapes with bulls and broncs over the years.

In his early years, he'd ridden both. But in the end, he'd had to admit he had more talent with broncs and stuck with that for the remainder of his career. It had been a year since he'd ridden his last bronc, and he honestly hadn't missed the tumbleweed existence of rolling into a different city every weekend. During that time of his life, he'd had no roots, only lots of aches and pains.

But it was good to see workers here that he'd grown

to know over the years. He could vouch for their skill at their jobs.

Who'd have thought with all the bulls and broncs he'd ridden, Larae would turn out to be his biggest challenge? And try as he might, he couldn't seem to focus on Jayda alone.

"Daddy!" Jayda's excited voice echoed across the distance between them.

Larae glanced over. He waved as Jayda bolted in his direction, and he scooped her up.

"It's gonna be the best rodeo ever. You know why?"

"Why?"

"Because Mommy's gonna be the queen who rides in with the flag at the beginning."

"She is?"

Larae's face went pink.

"Uh-huh. The queen she hired called in sick. But Mommy thinks she got a date and lied about being sick. Mommy was awful mad. Until Stella reminded her that her old rodeo queen outfit was still upstairs in the closet. Doesn't she look beautiful, Daddy?"

"She does." He couldn't tug his gaze away from her. It was if time had gone back on him. She looked just like she had in high school when he'd first fallen for her.

The staff broke up and went to their stations as Larae headed his way. The floodlights caught each sequin, sending glittery stars all around her.

"Mommy, Daddy said you look beautiful." Jayda's tone held awe.

Busted. The little stinker.

"Thanks." She shook her head. "I never thought I'd wear this again." Her gaze locked on his until she rolled her eyes. "But what do I do about the concession stand? I was supposed to work in it with Stella."

"I told you I'll help, Mommy."

"I know, Pumpkin, and I really appreciate it. But you won't be able to do as much with your cast."

"I can do it," Rance volunteered.

"Really?" Her gaze narrowed. "Don't you have to load more bulls for the second round?"

"Yes, but you'll be in the concession stand by the time I need to leave. We'll tag-team it."

"That sounds perfect. Except I'm too old for this." She looked down at her sequins with a grimace.

"Nonsense, you don't look a day older than the day I first saw you. In fact, you look exactly the same."

Shared memories hummed between them. And from the look on her face, they weren't all bad.

She glanced away first. "Well, I guess we better get to our posts. This show will be on the road before we know it."

"We're taking our rodeo on the road, Mommy?"

"No, sweetie. It's a figure of speech. It means the rodeo is about to begin." She kissed Jayda's cheek. "You stay with Daddy and help him in the concession stand. But remember to stay away from the grill. You get to put the pickles on the hamburgers."

"Okay, Mommy. And I'll remember to put the clear gloves on first."

"You'll be the best pickle slinger in the West." Larae shot her a wink and turned away.

A dozen hands watched her progress around the arena.

If he didn't win her heart back soon, some other cowboy just might take her away from him. He couldn't let that happen. *Wouldn't* let it happen.

He could not lose the love of his life. Not again.

Larae tightened her grip on the flag and waited at the entry gate of the arena as Denny finished announcing the order of events and told attendees where the bathrooms and concession stand were located.

The first chords of "God Bless the U.S.A." sounded as the gate swung open. She charged Molly into the arena, holding the flag high. Faster and faster as the final chorus built. As the song ended, she darted to the center of the arena and stopped. Strains of "The Star-Spangled Banner" began as the staff and small crowd stood, placing their hands over their hearts. Her throat knotted up. Patriotism was alive and well in Medina, Texas.

Maybe she could get an actual singer for the grand opening of the indoor arena. As the song ended, she waved and exited the arena, then hurried to the bathroom to change. She did not need mustard on her white jeans since she'd probably end up with this as a permanent gig.

"Ladies and gentlemen, welcome to grand opening of the Collins Family Rodeo, dedicated in the memory of Laura Collins." Denny's voice came over the loudspeaker. "Bow your heads with me, and let's bless the event."

The mention of her mom's name put a knot in Larae's throat as she closed her eyes.

"Dear Heavenly Father, keep all the cowboys, the pickup men, and the bullfighters safe tonight. Place Your hedge of protection around each event and keep injuries at bay with Your mighty hand. In Jesus' name, Amen."

Larae's eyes watered up. You didn't hear that at just any rodeo.

A few more spectators had arrived when she exited the bathroom and made for the concession stand, but there were still plenty of empty seats. She needed more attendees to make this thing work. Still, it was only the first night. If everything ran smoothly, with little downtime between events, word of mouth would travel and more people would come.

If only she didn't have the entire ranch riding on the rodeo's success.

She stepped into the concession stand. Stella manned the grill, while Rance took orders and money and Jayda dispensed pickles. Larae slipped behind Rance just as he turned to put cash in the box. He smacked into her, and bills went flying.

"Cleanup on aisle six." He grinned as he gave the customer change, then called the order out to Stella and went to work on a hamburger bun and condiments.

Jayda giggled. "I'll get it, Daddy." She scurried around the floor, picking up bills as Larae took her first order.

Everything was surreal as memories of her and Rance working in the concession stand together at the rodeo in Bandera surfaced. Only back then, if they ran into each other accidentally when she finished her queen turn or in between her barrel racing and his bronc-busting events, they stole kisses when no one was looking.

Rance finished his order.

"We've got this, if you need to go." She hoped he'd take the hint.

"I'm good. I can help out for another hour, then I'll need to go."

How could her heart take another hour of this constant proximity? Shifting back and forth behind each other, reaching for the same condiments with sparks flying every time their fingers touched, bumping into each other like awkward waltz partners.

They worked in tandem with a constant flow of hungry customers. At least they didn't have to make conversation. And they had company.

The rush ended, and Larae took a deep breath, leaning back against the freezer. "You did great, Stella. It's like you've fed a few hungry cowboys or something."

"Wow." Stella wiped her forehead. "I was getting worried that if it kept up like that, we might run out of food. We make a pretty good team. Especially Little Miss Pickle."

Jayda yawned.

"And you did great with your queen gig, Larae. You

looked like you did at sixteen. I knew that outfit would still fit you."

"It probably needs to be updated." Her cheeks heated.

"Nah. People love vintage." Stella waved a hand through the air. "I sure would hate to try to fit into something I wore when I was sixteen. I think we've got a pretty good crowd, though, for our first night."

"I don't know. There are lots of empty seats."

"They'll fill up. Just give folks time to learn about us. If there's one thing Texans love besides barbecue, it's a good rodeo." Stella patted her arm.

"I was thinking when we open the indoor arena, I could get a live singer. Maybe we need one now. A big name to draw people in."

"Garrett Steele and Brant McConnell live somewhere around Denton, don't they?" Rance frowned and rubbed his chin. "I think I read something about them both doing a concert for an animal shelter. Maybe one of them would come."

"That's a great idea. They actually did stints at the rodeo in Fort Worth, too."

"Who are Garrett Steele and Brant McConnell?" Jayda yawned again.

"We've heard them on the radio, Pumpkin. They're Christian country music singers. How about we go see if we can find Grandma and Grandpa to take you to the house?" She'd been distracted by doling out pickles during the first round of bull riding. But another round was coming, and it would probably be best if Jayda skipped it.

"I'm not sleepy." Jayda's words ended on a yawn.

"I'll take her." Rance checked his watch. "It's that time anyway. I need to see about some bulls."

"I don't want you seeing about bulls, Daddy." Jayda reached for him.

"Don't you worry none." He scooped her up. "I won't get in the pen with them."

"Did you know your daddy used to ride bulls?" Stella raised her eyebrows dramatically.

"He did?" Jayda was suddenly wide-awake.

"He sure did. And bucking broncs, too. Lots of those."

"I hope you won't do it again, Daddy." Jayda stuck her bottom lip out. "They're so mean."

"No worries. I'm done with all that. Now I just raise bulls for other cowboys to ride, and I stay out of their pens while I'm doing it." He shot Jayda a wink, then with a wave he exited the concession stand.

Was he really content with his life on the outside of the arena looking in? She hoped so. For Jayda's sake.

Rance held his breath and paced the office as Larae totaled the receipts. The racket of the adding machine pulled his nerves taut. Aside from the start-up costs, had they spent more than they'd taken in?

The adding machine went silent. She straightened the tape, checked it with her notes, then blew out a big breath. "With the checks I wrote out to staff and the purse we paid out, we cleared forty-three dollars. Of course, that's separate from the cost of construction."

"At least, we didn't go in the hole for the night."

"We barely cleared even. Forty-three dollars a night won't save the ranch."

He dug his check out of his pocket and held it out to her. "Here. You don't have to pay me."

"I most certainly do." She looked at the check as if it were a rattlesnake.

"Take it. I can wait until you turn a bigger profit."

"No." She gored him with a look. "You have employees to pay, and you provided excellent stock. I couldn't have done this without you."

A compliment? "Consider it my contribution to the rodeo. And besides, I want to help you financially with Jayda."

She studied the check and chewed on the inside of her cheek. "I guess if you put it like that." She took it, set it on top of the bills and checks from last night. "But just this once. Tonight, I'm paying you."

"As for the rodeo, these things need time. It typically takes two years for a new business to get out of the red."

"Yes. But the ranch doesn't have two years. I'll have to think of something." She turned to the computer, did some typing. "Like call Garrett Steele and Brant McConnell's manager."

She grabbed her phone and punched in the number. "Yes, this is Larae Collins. I've recently started a new rodeo in Medina and I know your clients, Mr. Steele and Mr. McConnell enjoy performing in their home state and helping out with local events, so I was wondering if either of them would be available some weekend soon." She listened for several minutes.

"I see. Yes, I know it's short notice. Well, I'm in the process of building an indoor arena. Our grand opening should be in a few months. Maybe we can work something out then." Her eyes widened. "Oh, that's perfect. Thank you so much. I'll be in touch with more details soon. Yes. Thank you." She hung up.

"One of them can make the grand opening?"

"Both. If we can have it the Fourth of July weekend. The venue they were booked with for that weekend had to cancel due to a tornado."

"Will it be open by then?"

"I'll just have to make sure it is. But that doesn't help me now."

"Did you fill out the paperwork to get professionally sanctioned yet? That will attract more competitors with bigger purses and a chance to improve their rankings."

"I got it yesterday, but I haven't had the time to fill it out yet." She stood and went over to the window. "You know, I came home to sell the ranch. But I didn't really want to. I just thought I had to because it was losing money. And because I felt I needed to keep Jayda a secret from you."

"You thought you were doing the right thing." With what she thought she knew of him, it made sense. Somewhere in between their arguments and peaceful moments, he'd come to terms with her keeping Jayda a secret from him. His heart had softened. He had forgiven her. And maybe himself. Somewhere over the last few weeks, he'd let go of his anger.

"I'm sorry." She caught his gaze. Sincerity was there in her pale blue, slightly glossy eyes. "I should have told you the truth."

"I'm sorry for the way I treated you."

They connected for a deep moment before she turned back to the window. "I really thought the rodeo would work."

"I still think it will. Just give it time."

"I told you, the ranch doesn't have time." She swiped her hand over her face.

Her tears had always been his undoing. He stepped behind her and gently placed his hands on her upper arms, totally expecting her to jerk away. Instead, she leaned against him as a tremble shook through her. Her turned her in his arms, and she pressed her face into his shoulder, soaking his shirt collar.

This was more than about the ranch—maybe some pent up grief over her dad, the stress of raising Jayda on her own all these years and him being back in her life. Plus the ranch situation. He kissed the top of her head.

She stilled, quieted and tilted her head back to look up at him. So shattered. Her gaze dropped to his mouth.

And it was all the invitation he needed. He claimed her lips tenderly, once again expecting her to pull away. But she didn't. Her response hammered his pulse into a frantic rhythm, filling the hollows she'd left in his heart after their breakup.

"Aha." Jayda giggled.

They sprang apart.

Jayda pointed a finger, her smile gleeful. "I knew you wanted to kiss her. Y'all should get married."

"Jayda." Crimson washed over Larae's face. "Sometimes people…accidentally kiss. That doesn't mean we're getting married."

Accidentally? He raised an eyebrow.

Larae's face went purple.

"But why not? Most parents are married. At least for a while. Why aren't y'all?"

"It's complicated." Rance tried to figure out a way to satisfy her. "God intended marriage to be forever. Not for a while. Before people get married, they need to be sure it's what they both want. Forever is a long time. It's not something to be rushed, Baby Girl."

"Okay, Daddy. But you and Mommy at least like each other, right?"

"I've always liked your mama. But even when people like each other, sometimes they disagree."

"And sometimes they kiss?" Jayda frowned, obviously trying to understand.

"Why don't you go see if Stella has lunch ready yet?" Larae squirmed visibly. "And then I need to fill out some papers to get our rodeo sanctioned."

"She's making lasagna. My favorite." Jayda scurried out.

All he wanted was his family whole. For Larae, the woman he'd loved since high school to stay in his life. For Jayda to be officially his daughter.

"Why don't we get married, Larae?"

"What?"

"No matter how much you protest, it's obvious the old fires are still there. And I want Jayda to have my name."

"Marriage isn't about fire or convenience, Rance." Hurt dwelled in her voice. "It's supposed to be about love, mutual respect and commitment. And to answer Jayda's question, half the time, I don't like you. You make me so mad I can't see straight." She stalked out of the room.

Great. Now he'd insulted her. She made him so mad he couldn't see straight, either. But amid the fire and smoke, there was love. He loved Larae. Always had and always would. The question was—how could he get her to fall for him again?

Chapter Twenty

Larae had done her best to avoid Rance, despite working in the concession stand with him again last night. The rodeo had cleared eighty-five dollars. And Rance had actually kept the check she gave him. Today she'd driven Jayda to church instead of riding with him. She could not allow herself to get reeled in by him and confuse Jayda even more.

After shaking the pastor's hand, she and Jayda exited the lobby and headed for her SUV.

"Mommy, can I go swing with Amelia for a minute?"

"Sure, sweetie."

Larae stopped under a shade tree and checked her phone for messages.

"Want to go on a road trip?" Rance was suddenly right in front of her.

"I don't need to put up any more flyers. I have to finish the sanctioning paperwork and get it mailed tomorrow. And what part of not spending so much time together did you not understand?"

"I do get it. But since I've put the last three weeks into the rodeo, I haven't spent much time on my own business. I have an appointment with the manager of the Mesquite Rodeo. I figure you know all the rodeo movers and shakers, and I was hoping you'd go with me and put in a good word for me."

She owed him that much since she couldn't have gotten her rodeo going so quickly without him. But riding in a truck to Mesquite and back with him. Alone. She squelched a shudder.

"I won't try anything, I promise. No pressure about our relationship. I just want you to vouch for me. That's all."

"That's ten hours on the road. A long day. What about Jayda? She has school."

"I sort of took the liberty of asking Mom and Dad if she can stay with them, and of course they said yes. They've been itching to ask you about a sleepover, but they didn't want to push."

"Your parents have been great about all of this." She looked toward the sky, trying to come up with another valid reason not to go. "The construction crew is starting on the interior tomorrow."

"They've got the plans. You don't need to supervise."

Besides all his help, he'd ended up providing stock for free on Friday night. "Okay. I'll go, but I have to make a few calls on the way. I need to check with my contractor about meeting the deadline so Garrett Steele and Brant McConnell can come for the indoor grand opening."

"I'll remind you. How's that?"

"What time do you want to head out?"

"I figure we can see Jayda off to school and leave after that."

"See you then."

What was she thinking? Ten hours on the road. With Rance. Confined in a truck. With Rance.

"Daddy." Jayda vaulted toward them. "Amelia's mommy said I can come to her house sometime after school or on a weekend if it's okay with y'all."

"I'm sure that can be worked out."

Why hadn't Larae thought of that? Because she'd been consumed with the rodeo instead of her daughter. Poor

Jayda. Since they'd moved to Medina, other than school and church, she'd spent all her time with adults.

"Maybe tomorrow?"

"I'll have to get in touch with Amelia's mom on that." Larae slipped her phone into her purse. "But tomorrow your daddy and I have to go on a business trip. We'll be gone all day long, but you'll be with Grandma and Grandpa until we get back."

"Yay. I mean—I'll miss y'all. But I'll have fun at Grandma and Grandpa's."

"And when I get home, things will be different." Larae pressed her hand to heart. "I promise not to be so busy with the rodeo, and maybe Amelia can come to our house, too."

"Okay, Mommy. But I've had fun helping you get ready for the rodeo."

"I'm so glad, sweetie. I've had fun, too." Larae's heart flipped over. The child required so little—only time and attention, even if Larae was on the phone and Jayda put a check mark by each staff member when they confirmed they'd be there or filed the contestants' online registration forms.

Maggie and Davis approached with smiles and waves.

"Guess what?" Jayda jumped up and down.

"You get to stay with us all day after school tomorrow. Until bedtime."

"Yippee. What are we going to do? Every time I say, let's go to the park or to play Putt-Putt, y'all always say we don't have time before I have to be home. But we do now."

"So which do you want to do?" Maggie asked. "You pick."

"Hmm." Jayda tapped her chin with her forefinger. "Let me think on it."

All this time, Larae had been so intent on not inconveniencing Maggie and Davis or making them feel taken advantage of and ensuring Jayda got plenty of mom time.

In the end, she'd put a leash on them, which was the last thing she'd meant to do.

"If you want—and only if it's okay with Grandma and Grandpa—you can go ahead and spend the night, too."

"That would be perfect." Maggie clasped her hands together. "We'd love that."

"Yay." Jayda jumped up and down. "Are we going to lunch at O.S.T.?"

"Sounds like we are." Davis laughed, completely enchanted. "We'll meet you there."

"Can I ride with Daddy, Mommy?"

"Why don't we ride together?" Rance suggested.

It was the last thing she needed, but she might as well get used to riding with him.

"Yay." Jayda bounced even more.

"Y'all go on. I'll lock my SUV and be right there."

Jayda grabbed Rance's hand, and they headed for his truck.

"I'm sorry." Larae ducked her head. "I didn't want to put y'all out with keeping Jayda all the time. And in the process, I've not given y'all enough time with her, have I?"

"It's okay." Maggie patted her arm. "Just know that we're happy to have her anytime. For as long as we can get."

"If it gets to be too much, you'll tell me."

"It won't."

"And y'all are truly welcome at the ranch anytime. For supper or fishing or whatever. I'm really glad y'all are in her life."

"Thank you, Larae." Maggie gave her a hug. "I can see why Rance fell for you back in high school. Davis and I are hoping y'all can work things out."

Her face went hot. "But we're not—"

"Just keep an open heart." Maggie patted her arm

again. "See you at O.S.T." She and Davis turned toward
their car.

Her open heart was the problem. Open hearts got hurt.
And Larae couldn't take having her heart broken again.
Yet, she'd agreed to drive to lunch with Rance. And tomorrow, on April Fools' Day, she faced a ten-hour trip
with the very man who'd shattered it. How fitting.

A country love song came on as they neared Mesquite.
"This reminds me of prom." The words took Rance right
back to dancing with Larae in his arms.

"No relationship talk."

"That's not where I was going with this." He took the
Mesquite exit. "Remember when Charles Bloomingdale
threw up on Florence Hightower's shoes."

Larae giggled. "The look on her face was priceless.
That's what she deserved for helping him sneak booze in."

"They both got suspended and had to attend summer
school before they could graduate."

"I wonder what happened to them. I never see anyone
we went to school with. Do you?" Larae asked.

"Most of them lived in Fredericksburg, but they've
probably moved on to bigger and better things by now."

"We didn't fit in, did we?"

"No. We didn't. Maybe that's why we hit it off. Oops.
Subject change. Well, looky there, we're here." He pulled
into the parking lot. The massive coliseum was as impressive as the first time he'd seen it.

Once inside the building housing the offices, she
scanned the names on the directory. "Here it is. Alejan-
dro Vega. This way."

"How did you know his name?" He matched her stride.

"He used to be my boss."

"Why didn't you tell me?"

"I don't know. I guess I didn't think it was important."

"It's very important. You're giving a good recommendation to someone you personally know and worked for. That means he'll listen to you." He put a hand on her shoulder, and she stopped. "You have no idea what this means to me."

"I figure I owe you. For all your free labor, free stock and a certain seven-year-old secret I kept from you." She grimaced. "But I won't mention the free-stock part. Special circumstances and a one-time thing."

Their gazes locked. "Thank you, Larae."

"I'm just making sure I get my child support." She gave him an impish grin. "Now come on, or we'll be late."

He followed, in awe of her once again. If only she could trust him on a personal level and not only professionally. He hoped that by sticking around, eventually he could win her over. And win her heart again.

"May I help you?" A receptionist sat behind a sleek desk.

"I'm Rance Shepherd. I have an appointment with Mr. Vega."

"Yes. Have a seat, and he'll be with you shortly."

Larae chose a seat, and Rance settled beside her. Tension pinged through him due to a combination of nerves over the meeting and being so close to Larae. And so far away all at the same time.

He tried to think of something else and couldn't. Her apple scent messed with his senses while her confidence in him messed with his heart.

"Mr. Vega will see you now." The receptionist escorted them to a door on her right.

He ushered Larae in first.

A graying Hispanic man stood from his desk. "Larae Collins, tell me you're here for a job." He grasped her hand with both of his.

"Um, no." She opened her mouth, started to say something, then closed it.

"But you're not at the rodeo in Fort Worth any longer?"

"No."

"I just learned this morning that my marketing director is getting married and leaving. She was supposed to stick with me through the current season, but her fiancé is in the military and being stationed across the country, so they moved the wedding up." He rubbed his hand over his face. "And then you show up, unannounced. It's like God is taking care of it for me."

"But I just started my own year-round rodeo in Medina. My first outdoor event was last weekend with an indoor arena under construction."

"You'd only have to work for me for six months. The rest of the year, you could concentrate on your rodeo."

"I'll think about it. But I'm not here about me. This is Rance Shepherd, my stock contractor. I wanted to recommend him."

"That name's familiar." Mr. Vega clasped his hand.

"I worked for John Leonard, sir. When he retired, I bought most of his stock."

"Leonard had a good outfit. Tell me about the bloodlines on your bulls."

Rance ran down the list he'd memorized.

"Impressive." Mr. Vega raised an eyebrow. "You got any numbers for me."

"Yes, sir." Rance opened his satchel-style briefcase and handed Mr. Vega a folder.

"I'll look over this and get back to you." He reclaimed his seat, gesturing for them to sit in the two chairs facing him. "Now about that job, Larae. I'll give you a fifteen percent raise above what that outfit in Fort Worth was paying you."

"I don't know what to say."

"Say yes."

Rance's heart hammered. He had to get her out of here. She couldn't move five hours away, even for six months out of the year. He liked having her right next door way too much to lose her.

"I live in Medina now on the ranch where I grew up."

"We're just talking six months. You could work four days here and the rest of the time at your ranch."

"I'll think about it and let you know."

"Think hard." He opened Rance's folder. "Y'all be careful driving back now."

"Thank you." Obviously dismissed, Rance stood and followed Larae out.

He hadn't brought her here to receive a job offer—a job that would take her away from Medina.

They retraced their steps and exited the building.

He waited until they got in the truck to broach the subject. "Please tell me you're not thinking about taking the job."

"If I decide I want it."

"But you'd either have to move here six months out of the year or spend all your time commuting."

"Yes. I'm a free agent."

"But what about Jayda? She loves it in Medina."

"She loved it in Dallas. She'd learn to love it here."

"But her schooling. She'd have to live half the year in one place and half the year in the other."

"You really don't have any say in the matter."

"I'm her father, and I love her." He couldn't lose her. Or Jayda. He'd do whatever it took to keep them both. Even if it meant not playing fair. "Don't make me use my pull on this, Larae."

Her gaze flew to his, fear in the blue depths. "Are you threatening to hire a lawyer?"

"That's not what I meant. My pull with Jayda. She loves me, loves living near me. If it was up to her, we'd all live together." If it was up to him, they'd be married by now.

The fear stayed in her eyes and tugged at his heart.

"I'll never try to take Jayda away from you, Larae. You're her mother. I just don't want you to move. But if you do, I'm moving, too. And not only because of Jayda. I love you, Larae. Don't you know that by now?"

She looked away. "I wish I could believe you. That there really is such a thing as a happy ending—well, there's not."

But there could be. He needed to find a way to convince her of it. But how? He'd bared his heart and she still didn't get it.

Chapter Twenty-One

Rance had said he loved her last night. Larae's heart stuttered. If only she could trust his words.

She hurried downstairs, hoping to relieve Stella of cooking breakfast for once. But when she entered the kitchen, Stella was already in her usual spot at the stove.

"You don't have to cook me breakfast, you know."

"I don't have many talents." Stella scrambled eggs with her spatula. "Let me share the one I have. So how was your road trip with Rance?"

"We got back in time for supper at his parents' house and visited with Jayda." Deep down, Larae had hoped Jayda might chicken out about spending the night there and want to come home. But she hadn't. The night had been far too quiet. And lonely.

"Any developments?"

"I got a job offer."

Stella's eyebrows raised. "I meant between you and Rance?"

"There's nothing to develop."

"You know I just want you to be happy." Stella plopped eggs on her plate. "What kind of job offer?"

"Marketing director in Mesquite. I'd work six months each year. I'd have to live there or do a lot of commuting during those months."

"What about the ranch?"

"It could run without me." But at the rate the rodeo was going, she still might end up selling. "I need a steady job, certain income. For Jayda's sake."

"You're far from the poorhouse."

"Yes, but I'd like to leave at least part of my inheritance to Jayda someday."

Stella pinned her with an unwavering gaze. "The rodeo will pick up. You could stay here. And open your heart."

"My heart is completely filled with Jayda."

"Someday, she'll be all grown-up and gone. You'll be alone. Rance loves you, and you love him."

"No, I don't." Larae managed a sarcastic laugh. "And he doesn't, either."

"You can deny it all you want. But y'all remind me of how Denny and I were, so stuck on each other we couldn't think straight. And you're just scared."

"Am not." Her response made her feel and sound childish, but it was all she could come up with.

"Are too. Afraid of getting hurt. I don't know what happened between y'all the first time. I didn't even know there was a y'all. But you obviously got hurt. Y'all were too young then. Now you're both older, wiser, more solid. You should give it another shot." Stella pointed the spatula at her. "I try to stay out of Lexie's and your business, but sometimes you young people need a voice of reason."

"I still love you, Stella. Thanks for breakfast," Larae said, though she had eaten little of it. "I have some work to do in the office." She nabbed a piece of toast and took her coffee with her.

If only Stella knew the whole story. Then she'd understand why Larae couldn't let Rance take up residence in her traitorous heart again. He'd burned her once. If she let him do it again, it was on her.

She sat down in her father's chair and picked up the flyer Garrett Steele and Brant McConnell's manager had faxed over so she could email it to the radio station. At least, if she couldn't get her outdoor arena off the ground, maybe her indoor venue would be a hit.

She soon realized no one had ever installed the scan function of the printer into the computer. Where would her father keep his software? She opened each drawer of the desk, finding a stack of discs in the bottom one.

When she picked up the stack, a loose disc slid out and became wedged in a crack at the base of the drawer. As she retrieved it, the wood pulled up with the disc. A false bottom. She flipped the wooden panel open to reveal a single sheet of printer paper folded like a letter.

Was this something she wanted to find? She hesitated, her heart hammering, and jerked her hand back as if she'd been burned. What if her father had some deep, dark secret?

No. Of course not. He had never kept secrets from her. Maybe legal papers. Something to do with the ranch. Or with her mother. A love letter to her mom. She smiled, picked up the paper, unfolded it.

"I, Rance Shepherd, do solemnly swear to stay away from Larae Collins—" she frowned and kept reading *"—in exchange for the sum of fifty thousand dollars."*

Her heart dropped to her stomach.

"I will not see, call, write, email or make any form of contact with Larae. I will not ask for more money at any time. This contract is a one-time offer, final and binding."

Her father's signature was at the bottom in his usual bold scrawl. The paper fell from her fingers and fluttered to the floor. She covered her face with her hands. Dad paid Rance off. That's why he had broken up with her. And probably why he'd quickly moved on to a string of other girls.

For fifty thousand dollars.

Rance had put a price on her head.

And so had her dad.

A knot lodged in her throat, threatening to cut off any air. She gulped as she sank back into the chair.

How had her father even known about them? How could he have done such a thing? How could Rance agree?

For money.

Had he only gotten involved with her because her family had money? Who had come up with the contract, her father or Rance? Which one of them had established her worth?

One thing was resoundingly clear, the two men she'd trusted with all her heart had sold her down the river.

Her father might not be here to get a piece of her mind.

But Rance was.

She grabbed the contract up from the floor and stormed out of the office.

Rance was at loose ends. Without all the rodeo prep and with Jayda at his parents', he had no reason to go to Larae's until after school. But he wanted to anyway. He paced the floor of his kitchen. Had she picked up the sponsor signs for the indoor arena yet? If not, he could offer to do that. As good an excuse as any.

He was heading for the front door just as someone sat on the doorbell. The constant ding-dong, ding-dong, ding-dong grated on his nerves. He opened the door and found Larae on his doorstep.

Crying.

"What's wrong?" His heart stuttered. Had something happened to Jayda? "Is Jayda okay?"

"She's fine. But I've come to the conclusion that you need to stay out of her life."

"What? I can't. I won't."

"Oh, you will." She let out an ironic laugh. "I'll have my lawyer write up a contract. If you stay out of Jayda's life, I'll pay you fifty thousand dollars."

His breath stilled. She knew.

"Or is that enough? Has your price gone up in the last eight years?" She jabbed a piece of paper at him.

He knew exactly what it was.

"I guess with inflation, maybe I should offer you seventy-five thousand."

"I don't want your money. I didn't want your dad's, either."

"Then why did you take it?" Her voice cracked. "In exchange for me."

"I didn't."

"Yeah, right. I found the contract, Rance." She shoved the paper at him.

The contract, an object that practically reeked of hate and distrust. The contract he'd hoped had long been burned. He took it and unfolded it. There wasn't anything he could do to save her father's memory for her now. She knew exactly what her dad was capable of.

"Look." He held it to face her.

"I read it." She glared at him over the top of it. "Trust me, once was enough."

"Look at the signature lines, Larae."

Her gaze narrowed as she focused on the contract. Both eyebrows went up.

"That's right. Your dad signed it. I didn't."

Fresh tears came, dripping on the contract she was never supposed to see.

Why on earth had Ray kept it?

"I'm sorry, Larae." He gently placed his hands on her upper arms, and she melted into him. For the second time in a matter of days, Larae Collins soaked his shoulder.

He drew her inside, shutting the door behind her. Comfort was all he could offer, no matter how right she felt in his arms. No matter how much her tears tore at his soul. No matter how much he wanted to make her feel better.

Comfort and only comfort. She was entirely too vulnerable, and he would not take advantage of her emotions and steal the kiss he wanted so badly.

Her tears eased, but then her lips touched his neck.

High voltage shot through him. An accident.

She did it again. Kissed his jaw.

"Larae?"

"Hmm?" Lips entirely too close to his.

"Stop." He hauled her away from him, taking a step back.

The rejection in her eyes almost did him in.

"It's not that I don't want to kiss you. Trust me, I can't even tell you how much I want to kiss you. But you're upset. And you might regret it later. I don't want that."

She nodded, turning crimson. "I'm sorry. You're right."

"Want to sit? Maybe talk about your dad?"

"No. Maybe sometime, but that'll just make me cry."

"Want to watch *Duck Dynasty*?"

"Huh?" She frowned.

"It always gives me a good laugh when I need one."

"Okay." She sniffled. "I could definitely use a laugh."

He ushered her to the couch, then searched through his DVD collection. "Any preference? I have all the seasons."

"It doesn't matter."

"Season five it is then." He popped in the disc. Way too tempting to join her on the couch. Instead, he plopped into his recliner and turned on the TV. The familiar theme song started up.

"Rance?"

"Hmm?" He looked over at her.

"Thanks."

"You're welcome." He felt like her hero and, for now, it was enough.

She'd stayed at Rance's laughing over the Robertson family until it was time for Jayda to come home. His house was stark, sparsely decorated, but clean and neat. Not the bachelor pad she'd expected at all.

They'd met Jayda at the end of the drive and gone fishing. He and his parents had stayed for supper and he had left shortly afterward. Without discussing the contract.

This morning though, once Jayda went to school, Larae intended to ask questions.

"Are you about done with breakfast, Pumpkin?"

"Uh-huh." Jayda popped the last bite of pancake into her mouth.

"Go get dressed and brush your teeth. Grandma and Grandpa will be here soon."

"Okay. Thanks for the yummy breakfast, Stella."

"You're welcome, Miss Pickles." Stella beamed.

Jayda was bolting up the stairs as the doorbell rang.

"I'll get it." Larae hurried to the front of the house and opened the door.

Rance, with his parents, thankfully. Because yesterday she'd practically thrown herself at him. Even with Maggie and Davis here, it was still awkward. Her face warmed.

"Talk him into it, Larae." Maggie gave her a pointed look. "I'm counting on you."

"Okay. I don't know what it is, but I'll give it a shot. Come on in. Jayda is almost ready."

"I'll tell you what it is." Davis's put-upon tone didn't fit him. "Maggie's esteemed parents invited us to their fiftieth anniversary party. Tomorrow. And why such late notice? We're an afterthought."

"Don't mind him." Maggie rolled her eyes. "I'll work on Davis if you'll work on Rance for me."

"I'll try."

"Don't waste your time." Rance harrumphed.

"I know they're…difficult. But they are my parents. I wouldn't be here if not for them, and they're getting older. They made the gesture to invite us, and we're going. Understood?"

Neither man complied.

"I'm ready." Jayda ran down the stairs.

"Careful, Baby Girl, you'll fall."

But by then Jayda was already at the bottom. "I won't, Daddy. I hang on to the banister real tight with my good arm."

Larae gave her a hug. "You have a good day at school, and if you want, you can spend an extra hour at Grandma and Grandpa's today if they don't have something else scheduled."

"We're all hers." Maggie mouthed a thank-you.

Jayda hugged Rance. "See you later, Daddy."

"Bye, Baby Girl."

Jayda raced out. With a wave, Maggie and Davis followed.

And the real awkwardness set in.

"So tell me about the anniversary party."

"They called last night, and the party's tomorrow." He sighed. "They're obviously hoping we won't come."

"Maybe not. Maybe they've been wrestling with themselves for a long time because they were *afraid* y'all wouldn't come."

He scoffed. "You obviously don't know my grandparents."

"Well, it seems important to your mom."

"I can't figure out for the life of me why. Dad worked for them. That's how he and Mom met. And they've pretty much ignored us since Mom and Dad got married. And now they expect us to drop everything and come to their highfalutin shindig in the middle of the day?"

He gave a frustrated shake of his head. "Who has a party at two o'clock on Thursday? I'll tell you who, my hoity-toity grandparents who think nobody has to work— that we all just sit around twiddling our thumbs and being idly rich like them."

"Why don't you tell me how you really feel?"

He snickered. "They just rub me the wrong way. Because they hurt my mom."

"Well, I think if you don't go, it will hurt your mom."

"I know you're right." He growled. "How do you women do that? Twist us around until we do what you want?" He snapped his fingers. "I know. You have to go with me."

"No." She shook her head. "I'm not intruding on a family party I wasn't invited to."

"You can be my plus-one. That's it." He crossed his arms under his chest, striking a stubborn pose. "I'm not going without you."

"Don't be ridiculous."

"Just think of my mom."

Maggie could use the support, and she'd been so good to Larae. "Oh, all right. What should I wear?"

"They'll expect the most expensive, tasteful, formal dress you own. But it would be funny if you bought something really cheap and totally unfashionable from a thrift store. I'll see if I can find a blue polyester suit from the seventies."

"No, you won't. You'll not embarrass your mom."

"You're no fun."

Now that the issue was settled, a question burned in her gut. "Why did you break up with me if you didn't take the money?"

"Wow, you cut right to the punch, don't you?" He settled on the couch.

She chose a wingback. "I barely slept from wanting to know."

"To be honest, there was some pride involved. It hurt to know your dad thought I only wanted your money. I dated those other girls to convince you we were through. But after graduation, I was determined no one would ever think I was after anyone's money again. The few girls I've dated since were dirt-poor."

His gaze caught hers. "But the main reason was because I was afraid if we stayed together and I married you like I wanted to, your dad would disown you, like my mom's parents disowned her."

Her breath caught, and her brain didn't get much past the part where he'd said he wanted to marry her.

"I broke up with you and tormented myself by dating those other girls I didn't want anything to do with so you and your dad would stay an intact family."

"Why didn't you tell me?"

"I didn't want to hurt you."

"You don't think it hurt when you broke up with me?"

"I couldn't ruin your relationship with your dad. He was the only family you had. You had him on a pedestal, and I wanted him to stay there. For your sake." His gaze held her prisoner. "And if I had told you, it probably would have tainted our relationship. You'd have grown to resent me for ratting out your dad."

He'd thought of her more than her dad had. "How did he even find out about us?"

"He followed you to the river when you snuck out. That night, we heard him hollering your name, and you ran back home."

She'd pretended to be looking for her cat and thought her father had believed her. "He never said a word."

"Not to you. He caught me by myself in the barn the next day. He fired me and tried to get me to sign the contract."

"I waited for you that night, but you never came." Her heart clenched, just as it had by the river all those years ago.

"The next day, I told you I'd quit the ranch. And—" He closed his eyes.

"That you wanted to see other girls." She swallowed the knot in her throat. "Why didn't you tell me the truth when I came back here? Especially after you realized Jayda was yours?"

"I didn't want to sully your memories of your dad."

"So you let me think the worst of you, for all these years?"

"I knew you'd be okay as long as you had your dad." He shook his head. "Of course, I didn't know about Jayda back then. If I had, I don't think I could have stayed away."

"I still can't believe Dad did such a thing." She covered her face with both hands.

"He thought he was doing the right thing. And look at his history. He'd fallen for Delia who only wanted his bank account. That had to hurt him. He just didn't want you to go through the same thing."

"I can't believe you have sympathy for him, after what he put you through. Put us through."

"I know that someday Jayda will grow up, and there'll be boys sniffing around. And if I think one of them is no good and snowing her over, I'm sure I'll do whatever it takes to keep her protected. That's all your daddy was doing."

"I guess you're right." She shrugged. "He went about everything all wrong, but his heart was in the right place."

"You okay?"

She nodded. "Thanks for being honest with me."

"It's about time. We've had too many secrets from each other. Let's be honest from now on."

"Sounds good."

"So we're good."

"We're good." She laughed. "We better be. Since we're going to an anniversary party together tomorrow."

"Don't remind me." He massaged the back of his neck, then stood. "I better see if my tux still fits. It's been a while."

"You own a tux?"

"I do. It comes in handy when schmoozing with investors and stock breeders."

"Hmm, not the image I have of you at all."

"Well, I'm hoping, since you know the truth now, that your image of me will change. For the better."

"It already has," she admitted.

"See you after school." He stopped by her chair. "We on for church tonight?"

"Wouldn't miss it."

He took her hand gently in his and kissed the back of it, sending a shiver through her. Then he walked away.

In the last twenty-four hours, everything had turned upside down. Her dad had turned out to be the bad guy. The one who'd let her down. The one who'd messed things up between her and Rance. While Rance made hard choices and bore the consequences of those choices all for her.

Could it be that he was the man she needed him to be? That he always had been?

Chapter Twenty-Two

The door opened to reveal Larae in a shimmering, flowy pale pink floor-length gown.

"Wowza."

She checked out his black tux with tails. "You clean up pretty good yourself. I can't believe your grandparents are having such a fancy party midday. Don't they know social rules? Formal wear is for evening."

"They think themselves trendsetters."

"We better get going." She took his arm. "How long's it been since you've seen them?"

"I honestly can't remember. I've never been enough for them. The whole pickup-truck-and-cowboy-boots thing is so beneath them."

"I'm sorry they treated you that way."

"Me, too."

She locked the door and he escorted her toward his truck.

"Would it be easier to get into my truck or your SUV in that dress?"

"Your truck is a chore to climb into in jeans."

"We'll take yours then. I've been thinking about either getting a running board with two steps or taking my lift kit out since you and Baby Girl came into my picture. Speaking of Jayda, Stella's all lined up to pick her up from school. Right?"

"Right. I never imagined you'd turn into a family man."

Was it his imagination or had her eyes just gone teary? "The grandparents will probably approve of your SUV more anyway."

"I don't know, it's just a GMC. We're not talking Lexus here."

"Anything's better than a pickup in their minds."

"It's ridiculous how many problems money and class have caused in both of our families."

"And sad." He opened the door for her, helped lift all of her dress in. "Mr. Vega called last night. I got the Mesquite contract."

"I knew you would. You've got great stock and could've gotten the deal without me."

For once, he was on equal footing with Larae. He officially didn't need her money, and no one could accuse him of using her ever again.

But more than that, he'd realized it really didn't matter what other people thought as long as Larae knew he loved her. Not her money. And since she knew about the contract and how he'd turned down her dad's offer, she knew money didn't matter to him.

The miles to San Antonio were filled with easy conversation. The difference in their relationship was like day and night. He liked this new ease between them. Maybe it could lead to something more. And maybe, just maybe they could start all over.

"It's clear." Larae looked out her passenger window as he took the exit. "I never asked where the party's being held."

"Why the Rose Hill Private Club of course, *dahling*." He did his best snooty voice. "Anybody who's anybody has a membership there."

She laughed. "Well I guess I'm not anybody then."

"I don't want to be anybody."

Several turns later, he pulled into the circle drive, then into the arched drive-through, where a valet scurried to open his door.

"Name please, sir."

"Terrance Shepherd." He held out his keys. "For the Remington anniversary party."

The attendant didn't take them until he had confirmed that Rance was on the list. Once approved, Rance opened the door for Larae, and the valet drove away.

"I had no idea your name was Terrance."

"Seems like there's a lot you don't know about me. But I'd like to be an open book for you."

She bit her lip. "How do they keep up with whose car is whose?"

"No idea. Maybe we can leave in a Lamborghini."

"You're so bad." She slipped her hand into the crook of his arm.

It fit just right, and warmth threaded through him.

Inside, the hum of rich and powerful small talk greeted them. His parents were already there, held prisoner by his grandparents at the head table. His mother waved them over.

"Oh my, Hayes, look at our handsome grandson." Nonna patted his cheek. Still as stiff and powdered as ever, with her hair in her usual tight French twist, she dared not smile for fear of wrinkles.

"And who do we have here?" His grandfather was a little less uptight, but not much. Tanned and toned, he played golf every day with the movers and shakers in real estate.

"This is Larae Collins."

"Of the Austin Collins?" Nonna's interest was piqued.

"No. Just a Medina Collins," Larae clarified.

"Oh." Nonna looked like she'd sucked on a lemon. "Well, what a lovely dress, dear. Too bad rose gold is so last year. I adore the color."

Rance's hands tightened into fists. "Let's sit down." He ushered Larae to a seat beside his mom, and whispered in her ear, "You're gorgeous in the dress. Nonna wouldn't know good taste if it stung her on her Botoxed cheek."

"It's okay. I used to go toe-to-toe with Delia Rhinehart and Evangeline Chadwick. And look at them now."

"I just don't understand why my grandparents have to be so condescending."

"Maybe their parents were the same way, and they don't know any better."

"They know better. They just don't care."

"Calm down and smile. For your mom." She clasped his hand.

Being here was worth it if he could hold Larae's hand all evening.

"Wait. A. Minute. Remington." She whispered, "As in Hayes and Cecelia Remington."

"That's them."

"They own half of—"

"Texas."

"I had no idea."

"How do you know who they are? You're not exactly a follower of the rich and famous."

"I get all the society papers and magazines so I knew who to hit up for funding whenever the rodeo in Fort Worth needed upkeep or repairs or sponsors. It was part of my job. I've probably hit them up at some point."

"I doubt you got anything out of them. Rodeo is so beneath them."

"I honestly don't remember, but you're probably right." She scanned the crowd. "I don't know a face here. But if I knew their names, I've probably heard of some of them. Do you?"

"Nope. Feeling like a fish out of water."

"So Davis, what is it you're doing these days?" his grandfather asked.

"I started my own real estate company. Remember?"

"Oh, yes. Small potatoes. What about you, Terrance?"

"Nobody really calls me that anymore. It's just Rance." He gritted his teeth. "And Dad's company is doing quite well."

"Are you working, Terrance?"

Completely ignored. As usual. "I just started my own stock contracting business."

"What in heavens is that?"

"I raise stock—bulls, broncs and steers for the rodeo."

"Still with the rodeo." His grandmother waved a dismissive hand through the air. "I thought surely you'd outgrow that nonsense someday."

"He's actually very good at what he does." Larae squeezed his hand. "I just started my own rodeo, and Rance provides excellent stock with great bloodlines."

"Bloodlines? Of bulls? Preposterous," his grandfather scoffed.

"Oh, but it's not." Larae's words came out pinched. She was obviously stewing over the way his grandparents belittled everyone they came in contact with. "It's not like it used to be when contractors bought bulls and hoped they'd buck. Now they're specially bred. A good bucking bull can sell for hundreds of thousands of dollars, and merely breeding one is even more profitable. Rance gets paid every time one of his bulls, broncs or steers leaves the chute. He has the beginnings of a multimillion-dollar company."

"Really?" Sarcasm dripped from Rance's grandmother's voice. "Breeding bulls?"

"And he just got the stock contract for the Mesquite Championship Rodeo. You might want to invest in Shepherd Stock Contracting. Or expand your own business interests."

"I think we're doing quite well." Rance's grandmother scanned the room. "Not just anyone gets to have their anniversary party here. They're booked for at least a year. But if you know the right people, strings can be pulled."

"What if some poor bride had to find another venue for her bridal shower?"

His grandmother's nose went higher in the air. "If she was having it here, she certainly isn't poor."

Larae gave a slight shake of her head. She'd gone toe-to-toe with Nonna longer than most. But obviously throwing in the towel, she turned to his mother.

"So how long have you and Davis been married, Maggie?"

"Going on thirty years."

"Wow. That's a long time. Congratulations."

"Thank you."

"So why can't y'all just admit that Davis is a fine man who married your daughter for love and be proud of your wonderful grandson?"

Everyone at the table went still, silent. Jaws dropped—including Rance's.

"I'm sorry." Larae pushed her chair back from the table. "I had no right to speak to y'all that way. I'll just be going now." She stood. "I'm so sorry, Maggie."

"Sit down, young lady." Rance's grandfather pinned Larae with flinty eyes.

"No. We're leaving." Rance stood and tugged on Larae's hand.

"Just hear me out."

Larae capitulated and reclaimed her seat, but Rance kept standing.

"I like her," his grandfather quipped. "I like a girl who speaks her mind. Especially since she's right."

Jaws dropped again. Including Rance's. And Larae's. He sank into his chair.

"Hayes, what are you saying?" His grandmother folded her napkin and set it aside. "This girl was utterly rude to us."

"Because we were rude to her. Pride has kept us from having a relationship with our Magdalena. And our grandson." He paused as he pursed his lips. "And our son-in-law. It's high time this nonsense ended, Cecelia."

His grandmother's face went purple all the way to the roots of her perfectly coifed silver hair.

"I'm sorry Magdalena—Maggie." His grandfather squeezed his mother's hand. She couldn't respond for her tears.

"Welcome to the family, Davis. Terrance—Rance. It's time we started acting like one."

"Hear, hear." His father raised his sweet tea glass.

They clinked their sweet tea glasses with his grandparents' champagne. Rance's grandfather stood and gave his daughter a hug, then Rance's father, and then Rance. "I'm glad you came tonight, Miss Collins."

"Thank you."

Rance's grandmother stayed seated. Obviously none of this was her idea, right down to the invitation. But maybe she'd eventually soften and come around. In the meantime, his mother had her father back.

And all because of Larae. In one evening, she'd single-handedly dispersed over thirty years of tension.

His family needed her. He needed her. Now how to go about winning her for good? That was the challenge.

Chapter Twenty-Three

After the opening ride finished, Larae paused for Denny's heartfelt prayer of protection, then changed out of her rodeo queen clothes and stepped inside the concession stand. Stella flipped burgers, Jayda dispensed pickles, and Rance manned the buns and condiments.

"Great news." He squirted a hearty glob of mayo. "Clay Warren is here. With his dad, Ty. And remember, Ty's a bull-riding legend, too. He won the championship four times."

"Really?" Her nerves went on high alert. From the good news or being near Rance? "Where?"

"Middle section, halfway up. His teenage daughter and wife are here, too." He pointed out the front window.

"I need to see if they'll do a radio interview. Maybe I could get the local station to come over."

"Or just a selfie with them on social media would probably do the trick."

"I'm going for both. Can you handle things here?"

"Sure."

"Is that the guy you went all silly about at O.S.T., Daddy?"

"Your daddy doesn't go silly over anyone but you." He tickled Jayda's ribs, sending her into a fit of giggles.

Larae grinned and headed for the door.

"Hey." Rance caught her wrist. "You were really great yesterday."

"What did you do yesterday, Mommy?"

"She set a couple of arrogant, condescending snobs straight."

"I don't know what all those big words mean."

"It means people who are rude and think they're better than everybody else."

"They don't sound very nice."

"They weren't, but they're nicer now. For the most part."

"And Mommy did that?"

"She sure did." He caught her gaze. "Your mama is amazing."

She could drown in his eyes, in his praise.

But she was on a mission. "Y'all hold down the fort. I'll be back."

"We'll be here." He shot her a wink.

And her heart fluttered.

She had to pull it together. Focus. She stepped out of the concession stand and headed for the bleachers. Several people had spotted Clay. By the time she reached his seat, he was posing for selfies and signing autographs. She hurried up the steps, maneuvering through his fans.

"Hi, Mr. Warren. I'm Larae Collins."

"I remember." He clasped her hand. "We met at the O.S.T. This is my wife, Rayna, our daughter, Kayla, and my dad, Ty."

"Nice to meet y'all. Thank you so much for coming to our rodeo."

"Was that you with the flag?" Kayla asked.

"It was. I hired someone for the position, but she had to bow out at the last minute, so I had to step in. Thankfully, I had a job as a rodeo queen in my teens, so I knew the ropes."

"It looked like fun."

"Well, maybe you can be my queen here when you get a little older."

"Awesome." Kayla flushed.

"I hate to ask." She turned her attention back to Clay. "I know you're just trying to have a nice evening of fun with your family." A line of fans snaked across the bleachers, still waiting to speak with them. "And it's already been interrupted."

"We're used to it. Part of our lives." He paused to autograph a teenage boy's T-shirt. "What do you need me to do?"

"If I can get our satellite radio host here, would you mind doing a quick interview?"

"Not at all."

"Thank you so much. We could really use the publicity."

"I'm happy to help. Just let me know if there's anything else I can do."

"You're being here is all I need. But since you asked, maybe a quick selfie for social media."

"No problem."

Larae took several shots of them together with his family. "Thanks so much. I hope ya'll enjoy the rodeo."

"I'm sure we will."

She hurried down the stands, Googled the radio station and made the call.

"KTEX FM, your Hill Country Radio Station for all things country. How may I help you?"

"Hey, Donna, this is Larae Collins."

"I heard you were back in town. And starting a rodeo on your ranch. How are you doing, girl?"

"I'm fine. We're up and running here at the Collins Family Rodeo, and I thought Ronald might want to interview Clay and Ty Warren tonight?"

"Both Mr. Warrens are at the rodeo?"

"They sure are. We'll be here until around eleven, but I'm not sure how late the Warren family will stay."

"Thanks for the tip. I'll let Ronald know and more than likely he'll be there in two shakes of a lamb's tail."

"Thanks, Donna." Larae hung up and managed to catch Clay's eye. She gave him a thumbs-up.

He returned her gesture, and she paused long enough to post the pictures with the Warrens on all of her social media sites, then tagged Clay and Ty Warren and her rodeo, before heading back to the concession stand.

"Did you git 'er done?" Rance asked, as she stepped back inside.

"Ronald Ashford is on his way, as we speak."

"Probably falling all over himself to get here." Stella grinned. "That boy does love a live interview with local celebs."

"I need another jar of pickles." Jayda placed her last four on a cheeseburger.

"Here you go, Baby Girl." Rance grabbed a jar from the fridge, opened it and forked her cold tray full of slices.

They worked for the next fifteen minutes or so as a steady line formed, with spurts of conversation and humor.

"Thanks for the tip, Larae." Ronald Ashford, with his ever-present recorder in hand, had stopped at the side window.

"You're welcome. He's in the middle section of the stands, halfway up."

"I see him."

"Can you plug my indoor grand opening? I wrote down the info." She handed him a note with dates and specifics.

"Sure thing." Ronald took off toward the stands with purpose.

"This could put our rodeo on the map, right, Daddy?"

"You're right, Baby Girl."

Larae lost track of time taking orders, filling them and

making change. When she looked up again, Clay and his dad were at the window.

"I can't thank y'all enough for doing the interview."

"It was fun." Ty scanned the menu. "It's been a while since anybody wanted to interview me. I'm old news."

"You'll never be old news, Mr. Warren." Rance managed to play it cool.

And Larae pressed her hand to her mouth to hold back a snicker.

"I'm really impressed." Clay leaned against the ledge of the window. "This is the most professional small-town rodeo I've attended."

"Thank you so much." If he kept up the compliments, Larae might get giddy over him, too.

The Warrens placed their orders, and she and Rance worked in tandem to fill them.

"It's on the house." With everything ready, she handed out two bags and a drink tray. "And anytime y'all can come, you've got free tickets and free food."

"Now, there's no need for that."

"Y'all may have put our rodeo on the map," Jayda piped in.

"I sure hope so. I think all rodeos should be on the map." Clay shot her a wink, then looked up at Larae. "Anything else I can do for you, you just let me know."

"Actually. Will you be here tomorrow night?"

"We're planning on it. In fact, I guess we better since we told the radio guy we were."

"Maybe before we begin, y'all could come to the center of the arena, talk up the rodeo for me."

"Consider it done." Ty tipped his hat. "We can sit at a table for selfies and sign autographs, too. That would keep people flowing better. It's kind of hard in the stands."

"You just don't know how grateful we are." Rance still couldn't shake his goofy grin. "We'll have a table set up for you."

"It's an honor. I've thought Medina needed a rodeo for years, so I'm glad it's finally happened and that it's being done well. Your little lady knows her rodeo stuff."

The Warrens waved and turned away toward the stands.

"He thinks y'all are married." Jayda looked from Larae to Rance. "I sure wish y'all were."

"Shh, we have other customers." Larae's cheeks warmed as she smiled at the woman next in line. "What can I get you?"

But, as she filled the order, she wondered what it would be like to be Rance's wife. Just as she'd dreamed of back in high school.

"I'm looking for the owner." A large man wearing a ten-gallon hat was next in line.

Larae offered her hand. "Larae Collins."

"I'm Billy Thornton. I used to be Clay Warren's agent, back during his title-winning years."

"It's nice to meet you, Mr. Thornton."

"I can see you're busy, but I have a client who's looking to buy a small rodeo in the area. And I must say I'm mighty impressed with what you're doing here."

"Thanks, but she's not looking to sell," Rance interrupted.

Larae shot him a glare. "Do you have a card?"

"I do." Billy passed her his business card. "Is your rodeo sanctioned?"

"The paperwork is in process, but I've been approved and should be finalized by my grand opening of the indoor venue."

"Perfect. My client will make you a good offer, so give us a call. We can talk about it, throw some numbers around in the six-figure range."

"Wow." Larae scanned the card.

"Call me." He turned toward the exit.

"But we don't want to sell, do we, Mommy?" Jayda pooched her bottom lip out.

"I don't know, Pumpkin. He mentioned a lot of money. I wouldn't have to take the job at Mesquite, and we could buy a ranch somewhere else."

"But it wouldn't be this ranch. And what about Daddy?"

"Don't you worry your pretty little head." Rance winked at Jayda. "Wherever you go, I go. But I'm with you on it, so maybe together we can convince your mama not to sell."

But if she sold, maybe she could eventually shake Rance. And keep her heart intact. Because even though he'd turned out to be completely different from the womanizer she'd thought he was, trusting him with a piece of her heart still terrified her.

At every turn, they argued. What if, in the end, they didn't work out? What if what they had was a teenage love—a love that never matured and grew up? If they tried again and ended up going their separate ways, Jayda would get caught in the crossfire. Larae couldn't let that happen.

A steady stream of people arrived for the Saturday night rodeo. More than they'd had so far.

Rance sat in the side window of the concession stand taking tickets and money, with Jayda helping him make change. Larae had been busy all day and keyed up over Clay and Ty Warren agreeing to brag on her rodeo tonight.

The Warren family had arrived early, and she'd given them a tour of the indoor facility and shared her future plans for RVs and campsites.

But Rance had to corner her after it was over tonight. They needed to talk. He couldn't go on like this anymore, with things up in the air between them. With her threatening to take a job in Mesquite or sell the ranch. They had to work things out once and for all. Make things official and permanent.

She'd been up in the announcer's booth with Clay and Ty. Waiting for things to get started. Keeping them contained until they made their announcement. She'd had him set up a table by the concession stand, with a marketing plan in place as usual, for folks to get autographs and then food.

The music started up with a couple dozen people still in his line. Definitely more attendees than they'd had so far. Maybe triple. With more competitors, as well.

Larae's horse vaulted into the arena. Carrying her flag in her spangled outfit, she was just as beautiful as she'd been in high school. Even more so. Especially since they were both Christians now. And they had a daughter. They needed to make this thing right and live happily ever after. His heart hummed just from looking at her.

"Sir." A man stuck his money in the window. "I need four tickets."

"Right. Sorry. I just love watching the flag." He tore off four tickets and handed them to the man before trying to concentrate on the next customer.

"You love watching Mommy, too. 'Cause you love her." Jayda put the money in the metal box.

"You're right, Baby Girl. I sure do." His insides warmed at the admission.

Stella arrived to cook. "We've got some crowd tonight." She tied her apron on. "I hope we don't run out of food."

"We shouldn't. Larae ordered extra last week."

"That girl lives on faith. I'm glad it's panning out for her. She's worked so hard on this."

"Me, too."

She lived on faith. Except where he was concerned. Larae had zero faith in their relationship.

The national anthem started up, and the people still in

line stopped to salute. Rance placed his hand on his heart, as did Jayda and Stella. The song ended, and Denny said his nightly prayer. After the amen, Rance went back to ticket selling as Larae vaulted her horse toward the exit.

"Ladies and gentlemen." Denny's voice came over the loud speaker. "Welcome to the Collins Family Rodeo."

Came in handy to have a former rodeo announcer as Larae's ranch foreman.

"You might ask, what makes it family? Well, I'm here to tell you—we've got a fully stocked concession stand, but there's no alcohol sold or served here in honor of Laura Collins. And tonight, we've got a really special treat for you. Anybody familiar with the name Ty Warren?"

The crowd went wild.

"How about Clay Warren?"

The crowd went wild again, and Rance let out a whoop of his own.

"Well, boy howdy, y'all are in for a treat tonight. Ladies and gentlemen, Miss Larae Collins, our owner, made all of this possible." Denny paused as a round of applause went up.

Still wearing her flashy outfit, Larae hurried to the center of the arena, waving and blowing kisses as she went.

"Mommy looks so pretty."

"She sure does." Rance had to swallow the lump the sight of her put in his throat.

"Welcome, everyone." Larae spoke into the microphone she held, completely at ease. "Thank you so much for coming. This rodeo has been a labor of love, and seeing the stands so full tonight warms my heart. Just to keep you up to speed, our indoor arena is currently under construction as you can see." She gestured to the building.

"With a grand opening date of July Fourth, we'll have some big names that night, so mark your calendars. We'll get started a little early at six since Christian Country artists Garrett Steele and Brant McConnell will be here for a mini-concert."

The crowd roared.

"That's right. I'm excited, too. And Mr. Clay Warren just confirmed that he'll ride a bull for us that night. Not to compete, just as an exhibition, and to inspire all our bull riders."

The crowd roared again.

"Now, Mr. Denny Parker has a special introduction. Back to you, Denny."

"It just keeps getting better and better." Denny let out a whoop. "Y'all are fixing to be real glad you came. Because tonight, we have none other than Texas's very own father and son duo. Yes that's right, we have with us in this very arena, four-time Champion Bull Rider—*Ty Warren.*" Denny's voice echoed through the night. "And with Ty is his son, also a four-time CBR champ—*Clay Warren.* This father and son duo of bull-riding legends are here tonight at the Collins Family Rodeo."

Clay and Ty ambled out to the center of the arena with Larae as cheers and whistles filled the night air.

Larae waited until the applause died down. "We're so glad y'all could be here with us tonight. Welcome to the Collins Family Rodeo." She passed the microphone to Ty.

"Thank you, Larae. Clay and I came last night to check this place out, and I'm very impressed. This is the most professionally run small-town arena I've seen." He passed the mic to Clay.

"I'm impressed with the bulls." Clay wiped his brow. "Did y'all see the one they call You Ain't Gonna? Now that was a bull. Made me kind of glad I'm retired."

The crowd laughed.

"I asked around till I found out the stock contractor's name." Clay continued. "A Mr. Rance Shepherd of Shepherd Stock Contracting. He's over in the concession stand serving up the best burgers I've had in a while grilled up by a lady named Stella Parker, who just happens to be our announcer Denny's wife. So, see folks, it's a real family rodeo, for more reasons than one."

Stella blushed as Rance applauded her. "Oh, stop."

Ty took the microphone again. "You folks have a good time tonight. Just so you know, Clay and I will be over by the concession stand signing autographs. And if you want, we'll do this newfangled selfie thing, too." He passed the microphone back to Larae.

"Just one more announcement." Larae sparkled from head to toe. "Our indoor rodeo will be CBR sanctioned. So tell all your professional rodeo friends about us. Now let's get this party started."

"Let's give 'em a big hand, folks." Denny stirred the crowd into a frenzy as Larae and the Warrens headed for the arena.

This would definitely put their rodeo on the map, making all of Larae's dreams come true.

Now it was his turn. And his dream was her.

Chapter Twenty-Four

The last floodlight went dim. The rodeo was over for the weekend, and tonight had been their most successful evening so far. The crowd had steadily grown since Ronald Ashford had aired Larae's gig with Ty and Clay Warren live tonight.

Maggie and Davis had taken Jayda to their house to spend the night, and Larae was itching to count her cash box.

"Whoa, there." Rance's voice came out of the darkness. "We may be in Medina, Texas, but it's not a good idea to go carrying around a cash box without a bodyguard."

"Everyone's gone. I think it's safe. You can go."

"What if I don't want to go? Ever? What if I want to be your permanent bodyguard?"

Oh, the things he did to her pulse. "It's late, Rance. We have church in the morning. And I'm too tired for banter."

"I'm not bantering. You've got some serious offers. From the rodeo in Mesquite. From Billy Thornton. And those are your decisions. Whatever you decide, I'll support you, but I want to put another offer on the table." He took the cash box from her. "Sit down."

She settled on the bottom bleacher.

He sat beside her and took her hands in his. "Whatever you decide about the ranch, I want to be in your picture. Not just as your stock contractor. But as your guy. And, eventually, as your husband. I want us to be a permanent fixture. A family."

"I don't know, Rance." She looked down at their hands.

"Why? You still have feelings for me. What's holding you back?"

"What if we give us a fresh try, we get all cozy, and it doesn't work out? We're not the only ones in the equation." Her gaze met his. "I don't want Jayda disappointed. Or hurt."

"Why wouldn't we work out? I love you. And you still love me, don't you, Larae?"

She squeezed her eyes shut. "Yes."

When she opened them again, he wore a goofy grin. "Then we'll make it work out."

"A relationship takes work. We argue. A lot."

"But we argue because we're fighting our feelings. Or playing tug-of-war over Jayda. If we give in and love each other, become a family, there's nothing left to fight about."

"I'm just so scared."

"I know." He cupped her cheek in his callused hand. "The most important things in life are scary. Giving your heart to another person. Trusting that person. But you can trust me, Larae. I didn't willingly break your heart eight years ago. And I won't break it again. It's time to make our happily-ever-after come true—eight years later."

Her heart's desire within her grasp. All she had to do was take it.

Tears rimmed her lashes. "I'm in."

He gently drew her to him. And she had the rest of her life to drown in those eyes. Eight years of kisses, tears and missing each other erupted between them. Until he pulled away.

"That's better." He kissed the tip of her nose. "Now that that's settled, do you know what you're going to do about the rodeo?"

"I only considered Mesquite because I wanted to run—from you. Same thing with selling the rodeo."

"No more running."

"The only thing I plan to run is our rodeo. Right here in Medina." She set her hand on the cash box. "I'm dying to know how we did tonight."

"It doesn't matter. We won the greatest prize of all." He kissed her again. Until she forgot all about the rodeo.

Epilogue

The grand opening of the indoor arena was off the charts as Garrett Steele and Brant McConnell wrapped up their final song. Her dream come true. The complex was immaculate, with bleacher seating and all of the sponsor signs they'd worked so hard to get in place.

"This place is practically standing room only." Larae sat astride her horse outside the arena with Rance by her side. "I hope it's like this when we don't have big-name singers."

"Good news." He stroked Molly's velvety cheek. "Garrett said he and Brant are retiring from touring. Sounds like they're interested in alternating weekends here with us."

"That would be awesome."

"They said to call their agent this week and work out the details."

"Jayda's waving from the concession stand." She waved back, and Rance did, too. The only person happier than they were was Jayda, who was past ready for a wedding, anticipating being able to wear the bracelet Rance had bought her.

The first notes of "God Bless the U.S.A." started up.

"That's your cue."

The gate opened, and Molly vaulted into the arena as Garrett Steele sang the patriotic words. The music built, and she rounded the arena faster and faster, then sped to the center as the final chorus ended. The arena went silent for a few seconds until "The Star-Spangled Banner" started up. Everyone stood and placed their hands on their hearts as Garrett's rich baritone did the anthem justice.

The song ended, and she turned Molly toward the exit.

"Hold up, Larae." Denny's voice came over the loudspeaker. "We've got one more special treat for y'all here at our grand opening tonight. Give our rodeo queen, Miss Larae Collins, the little lady who made all of this possible, a big round of applause."

The crowd clapped and whooped as she waved. Movement at the gate caught her eye. Rance was walking toward her, with one of the hands.

"Just stay put," Denny instructed.

"What's going on?" she mumbled. But with no microphone and the cheering of the crowd, no one heard her.

Molly shifted her weight, not used to standing in the arena for so long.

The hand reached for her flag, and Rance gestured for her to climb down. She did, and the hand took Molly's reins and walked her toward the exit.

"What are you doing?"

Rance grinned and spoke into a handheld microphone. "Ten years ago, I fell in love with a rodeo queen."

Why was he telling the crowd that?

"Back then, she ran barrels, and I rode broncs. We worked in the concession stand together and stole kisses around the side of it." Laughter swept over the crowd. "Life happened, like it tends to do, and we ended up going our separate ways. Now that rodeo queen owns this rodeo, and I'm a stock contractor. We work in the concession stand together, and I'm still in love with her."

A flush warmed her face.

"And the really good news is, she's still in love with

me." He dug in his pocket, pulled out a velvet box and dropped to one knee.

Larae's breath froze in her lungs as the crowd went wild.

"Larae Collins, will you do me the honor of finally marrying me?"

She nodded, tears threatening to cut off any words.

But he stuck the microphone in her face.

"Yes." It came out soggy but audible.

The crowd erupted as he slipped the ring on her finger, then stood, picked her up and twirled her around.

When he set her down, she was dizzy and weak-kneed.

"I may have swept her off her feet." He steadied her and pulled her into his arms as whistles and whoops echoed around them.

Once she recovered her balance, they walked hand in hand to the exit.

Workers, competitors and spectators congratulated them as they made their way out of the arena and toward the concession stand.

Jayda vaulted toward them, and Rance knelt to pick her up. "Y'all are finally getting married."

"We sure are, Baby Girl."

"When, Mommy? When?"

"I'm not sure, sweetie, but you can be our flower girl."

"Yay."

They reached the concession stand, and Rance set Jayda down. "You go on. We'll be there in a minute."

"Where are y'all going, Daddy?"

"I'm gonna steal some kisses from Mommy." He tugged Larae around the side of the stand.

Jayda giggled and disappeared inside.

"Just to clear things up, you've never had to steal my kisses." Larae stood on tiptoe.

He claimed her lips, soft and slow, then pulled back. "Big wedding or small?"

"Small. Family and close friends. At our church."

"Let's do this wedding thing tomorrow."

"Tomorrow?"

"I'm tired of waiting."

"It's only been two months since we officially got back together."

"You're wrong, Larae Collins. I've been waiting for you for eight years."

"Then let's not wait any longer. If the church is available, tomorrow is the perfect day for a wedding."

"Good answer." He claimed her lips again.

And his kiss erased eight years of heartache.

* * * * *

Look for the next book in
the Hill Country Cowboys series
by Shannon Taylor Vannatter,
available July 2020 wherever
Harlequin Love Inspired books
and ebooks are sold.

Addie kept monopolizing Evan's time. First at the B and B—though she could hardly blame herself for that. He was the one who'd insisted on helping her out. And now again at church. Surely he had better places to be than with her.

"Do you need to go?" she asked Evan. "Sorry I kept you so long."

"I'm not in a rush. I might pop out to Wilder Ranch for lunch with Jace and Mackenzie. After that I have to…" Evan groaned.

"Run into a burning building? Perform brain surgery? Teach a sewing class?"

Humor momentarily flashed across his features. "Go to a meeting for Old Westbend Weekend."

What? So much for some Evan-free time to pull herself back together. "I'm going to that, but I didn't realize you were. The B and B is one of the sponsors for the weekend." Addie had used her entire limited advertising budget for the three-day event.

"I thought my brother might block for me today. Instead he totally kicked me under the bus as it roared by. He caught Bill's attention and volunteered me for the hero thing." The pure torment on Evan's face was almost comical. "I want to back out of it, but Bill played the 'it's for the kids' card, and now I think I'm trapped."

"Look, Mommy!" Sawyer ran over to them. A grubby, slimy—and very dead—worm rested in the palm of his hand.

"Ew."

At her disgust, Sawyer showed the prize to Evan. "Good find. He looks like he's dead, though, so you'd better give him a proper burial."

"Yeah!" Sawyer hurried over to the patch of dirt. He plopped the worm onto the sidewalk and told it to "stay" just like he would Belay. That made both of them laugh. Then he used one of the sticks as a shovel and began digging a hole.

"He's like a cat, always bringing me dead animals as gifts. I'm surprised he doesn't leave them for me on the doorstep."

Evan chuckled while waving toward the parking lot. She turned to see his brother and Mackenzie walking to their vehicle.

"Do you guys want to come out to Wilder Ranch for lunch? I'm sure they wouldn't mind two more. It's a happy sort of chaos there with all of the kids."

Addie's heart constricted at the offer. No doubt Sawyer would love it. She wanted exactly what Evan was offering, but all of that was off-limits for her. She couldn't allow herself any more access into Evan's world or vice versa.

"We can't, but thanks. I've got to get Sawyer down for a nap." Addie wasn't about to attempt attending a meeting with a tired Sawyer, and she didn't have anywhere else in town for him to go.

Evan's face morphed from relaxed to taut, but he didn't press further. "Right. Okay. I guess I'll see you later then." After saying goodbye to Sawyer, he caught up with Jace and Mackenzie in the parking lot.

A momentary flash of loss ached in Addie's chest. A few days in Evan's presence and he was already showing her how different things could have been. It was like there was a life out there that she'd missed by taking the wrong path. It was shiny and warm and so, so out of reach.

And the worst of it was, until Evan, she hadn't realized just how much she was missing.

Don't miss
Her Hidden Hope *by Jill Lynn,*
available May 2020 wherever
Love Inspired books and ebooks are sold.

LoveInspired.com

LIEXP0420